MEREDITH INTO THE FIRE

SECOND EDITION

THE MEREDITH SERIES
BOOK THREE

AMANDA GALE

The fire i' the flint
Shows not till it be struck.

— WILLIAM SHAKESPEARE

CONTENTS

CHAPTER ONE

THE GRAY FOX

The beginning of March came with warm, clear weather, and Meredith began to feel the relief of spring. The sun in her face helped cheer her. It made up in part for the fact that she was now an outcast in her neighborhood. No one had made an effort to talk to her since her conversation with Jodi. They hadn't ignored her, hadn't been rude—they always waved at each other as they passed on the street or hopped in and out of their cars. But the intimacy was gone. Meredith resigned herself to the fact that she was alone.

She had seen Wes a few times since their breakup. They had run into each other before work, as they had before they began dating. For the first few days, each had pretended the other hadn't existed. But then one day they began to wave hesitantly, with expressionless faces. Each time, Meredith felt her heart lurch with longing. It seemed only right that he should be kissing her goodbye.

Tara drove in Friday afternoon so she could join Meredith for her weekly dinner with Henry and Katrina, who had insisted on taking them out to a fancy restaurant in Washington, DC, in honor of Tara's visit and to cheer Meredith up. Everyone met at

Henry's townhouse, and Henry drove them into Washington, easily navigating the city streets until he pulled up to a restaurant Meredith had heard of before. She couldn't prevent a grin from creeping onto her face. The restaurant was The Gray Fox, the executive chef of which was Shane Thayer. It seemed Chef Thayer was somehow destined to haunt her forever; she couldn't escape him.

"I know this place," Meredith said as they pulled up to the front of the restaurant, waiting for a valet to park Henry's car. "Chef Thayer was the star of that show I went to see with Vince and Nick." She remembered the way he had condescended to the competing chefs. "I didn't care for his attitude. Also I cooked one of his dishes for Wes. It didn't do it for me."

"Well, attitude or no attitude, this is one of the hottest restaurants in town," Katrina replied, looking through her window. "I'm psyched!"

Regardless of her preconceptions about Chef Thayer, Meredith was excited too. She had heard a lot about The Gray Fox since Chef Thayer had begun to make a name for himself, and she was eager to see what all the fuss was about. As she watched elegantly dressed people walking in and out, her spirits began to lift slightly.

They were shown to their seats toward the middle of the room, in which everything but the tables was oversized. Gigantic paintings hung on the cream-colored walls, and magnificent red drapes billowed over picture windows that ran almost from floor to ceiling. A baby grand piano sat on a raised platform in the corner, though no one was playing it at the moment. Ivory candles sat on each table. With a pang Meredith imagined herself and Wes here, sitting at one of the tables for two off to the side. This was just the kind of place he would appreciate.

They ordered wine and appetizers and began some light-hearted conversation until their entrées arrived. Meredith did not see why everyone made such a big deal over The Gray Fox and

Chef Thayer. She enjoyed her dinner but felt it was unimaginative and without soul. She had whipped up better dishes at the last minute in her own kitchen. She kept her opinions to herself, though, not wanting to mar the upbeat mood of the evening and recognizing that her own dark mood could be coloring her judgment.

Applause erupted around the grand open room. Meredith looked up and was surprised to find Chef Thayer himself entering the room from the kitchen. She wondered why he was making a personal appearance, then remembered that his show had been canceled after very few episodes. She wondered if he was trying to get back in the game, to appear before the public to increase the level of excitement surrounding his name.

As she had the night of the pilot, Meredith noticed Chef Thayer's thick, brawny frame; he looked powerful, imperturbable, and impassable. She doubted many people gave him a hard time about anything. The muscles of his arms were noticeable even at this distance, even through his white chef's coat, and Meredith imagined that he made cooking look easy, whisking with speed and slamming skillets onto a hot stove. But his chestnut hair was a little too styled, one curved crest hanging on either side of his face, falling just short of his ears, and he appeared to look not at people but through them, the smile on his face a little too cold.

She thought he was going to introduce himself to more prestigious guests, but to her surprise he instead made his way toward the piano, to the delighted gasps of everyone in the room. She watched as, with an exaggerated bow and a plastic smile, he seated himself before it and began to play.

Her feelings about him warmed at the first note, for it was obvious from the moment his fingers touched the keys that he was naturally gifted. Meredith was moved by the grace and skill with which he played, the swiftness with which his fingers glided across the keys and the sweeping gestures that propelled the dramatic melody. He looked commanding and capable, his head nodding here and there at the more vigorous bars. Meredith's gaze moved to his face. His lips were drawn into a stern smile, suggesting concentration, but his eyes were wide and his brows raised, giving his expression the appearance of ease and even amusement. Meredith realized that this was easy for him, that he knew he was impressing his audience and that the entire show had been fabricated to do so. Now the music sounded passionless to her, the product of someone who exploited his talent for the purpose of self-aggrandizement—much like his food.

Chef Thayer completed his performance with a sweep of his arm and sat for a moment to wait for the applause. When the guests began standing and clapping, he made the necessary rounds, shaking hands and patting backs, leaning over tables briefly with a show of making sure people were enjoying themselves.

Meredith turned back to her friends. They were clapping and chattering gaily.

"I will say this for Chef Thayer," Henry was saying. "He certainly knows how to put on a good show."

"I just can't believe he's out here," said Katrina. "I wasn't expecting to see him."

"Tom will get such a kick out of this when I tell him," Tara exclaimed. "He loves *The Gourmet Channel*. I don't know if he knows who Chef Thayer is, though. I'd never heard of him until you told me about him, Meredith." She turned to Meredith. "Honey, are you okay?"

Out of nowhere Meredith had been hit by a wave of sorrow as she remembered the last time she had seen Chef Thayer and the enchanting evening she had spent with Nick in Framington after. That night she had felt that a world of possibility lay before her, that she had been awakened after a period of darkness. Now, having suffered two more losses, she was resigned to the darkness, understanding how naive she had been to believe in happy endings. She thought of how much had changed in a year and a half, and she sighed.

She glanced up at her friends. All three of them were looking at her with eyes full of sympathy.

"We know you're a little preoccupied, and it's okay," Katrina said, and took her hand. "It must be hard for you. You just broke up with Wes a couple of weeks ago."

Meredith attempted a smile but did not respond.

Chef Thayer was trying to head back to the kitchen but was being held up by eager guests who wanted to shake his hand, compliment him on the restaurant, or ask for his autograph. He was attempting to keep his time short with everyone and obviously was beginning to grow bored with hobnobbing. He was kept for a long time at the table next to theirs. With a start Meredith realized that seated there was another well-known chef, one she had seen on *The Gourmet Channel* many times. She wondered if this chef's presence was the reason for Chef Thayer's overblown performance.

Meredith turned to her friends and sighed again. She was just getting ready to excuse herself and head to the restroom to splash some water on her face, hoping to perk herself up and extract herself from her memories, when Tara pulled on her arm and leaned in toward her.

"Chef Thayer is staring at you," she said.

Meredith looked up toward the next table, where she saw that Tara was right—Chef Thayer was indeed staring at her. His face wore a soft smile. He was completely ignoring the other chef's wife, who was in the middle of a tale she appeared to find very exciting. He seemed oblivious to his own rudeness, unconcerned by the fact that he was neglecting his guest and unembarrassed by his unyielding scrutiny of Meredith. Meredith was puzzled. She met his gaze, her expression blank.

Chef Thayer patted the chef's wife's arm and clapped the chef on the back, excusing himself and approaching Meredith's table.

Henry, Katrina, and Tara sucked in their breaths and opened their eyes wide as he approached. He stood between Henry and Katrina, his back straight and tall, his brawny frame looking imposing so close up. He rested one large hand on the back of Henry's chair, the other on the back of Katrina's, and looked down at them with a practiced smile.

"And how is everything tonight?"

"Wonderful," Katrina exclaimed. "Thank you so much."

"I'm so glad you're enjoying yourself."

"Yes, I'm very impressed," Tara said. "Everything was spectacular."

"Fantastic," Henry agreed.

Chef Thayer turned his attention to Meredith. "And you, ma'am? Was everything to your liking?"

Meredith couldn't bring herself to be part of the show. "It was good," she said, mustering a weak smile.

"That's it?" asked Chef Thayer, evidently noticing her lack of enthusiasm. "Just 'good'?"

Meredith was taken aback. "It was good," she said again. "It was fine."

"It was *fine*," Chef Thayer repeated. He placed his hands on his hips. "Is that 'fine' as in 'of superior quality,' or 'fine' as in 'passable'?"

Meredith stared at him. "It was decent," she said. "It was fine." The divot between her eyebrows wrinkled with thought; maybe she was imagining it, but this seemed to be about his ego, and she wasn't in the mood. "It wasn't exceptional."

Chef Thayer's eyebrows rose with interest. Henry's, Katrina's, and Tara's forked downward with disapproval.

"Oh?" Chef Thayer asked, shifting his weight. "Was there a problem?"

"No," Meredith said, shrugging her shoulders; if he wanted to do this, she would do it. "It just wasn't the best trout I've ever had."

"Really," Chef Thayer said, cocking his head. "And what would you do to improve it?"

"I'd add cilantro. It would complement the lime."

Henry, Katrina, and Tara were glaring at her with expressions of horror. Tara began shaking her head.

"Interesting," said Chef Thayer, though the look on his face told her he didn't find it interesting at all. "And what is your training, Miss—"

"Beck," Meredith told him. "Meredith Beck. I don't have any formal training." *What kind of question is that?* she asked herself, crossly. "I rely on common sense."

"Oh, my God," Tara muttered beside her. She leaned in toward Meredith and whispered, "What the hell are you doing?"

"No, no," Chef Thayer said brightly, his eyes locked now on Tara, his expression relaxed and good-natured. "I appreciate the input. We're always looking for ways to better please our guests." He turned his attention back to Meredith. "I'm glad you shared your opinion, Miss Beck. We'll take it under advisement."

"It's my pleasure," Meredith said, and smiled.

Chef Thayer was about to make his escape when, feeling oddly bold, Meredith called him back.

"You know, I made your meatloaf. It didn't quite turn out."

Chef Thayer turned back toward her.

"What was the matter with it?"

"The texture was unpleasant. It was rather dense."

"How far in advance did you prepare it?"

"I prepared it just before I cooked it, of course."

"When did you add the salt?"

Meredith hesitated. "I added it as I prepared it."

"There's your problem. You should have salted the meat in the morning, then let it sit until you prepared it that night."

"The recipe didn't say that."

"The recipe assumes that's understood."

Meredith blanched. She knew he was right and wondered how she had missed that.

"I'm very sorry you were dissatisfied with it, Miss Beck. I don't like making a bad first impression." He grinned, evidently trying to look dashing but looking goofy instead.

"It's okay. My boyfriend liked it."

Chef Thayer's face lost some of its luster. "Oh, I'm glad to hear it."

"Of course he and I disagreed about a lot of things. We broke up two weeks ago."

Chef Thayer's face now lightened. "How sad. I'm sorry for your loss."

Meredith stared at him curiously.

"Well, it was very"—Chef Thayer paused, his eyes lifted toward the ceiling as he searched for the right word—"*informative* talking to you. I hope you enjoy the rest of your evening."

He nodded around the table, then rested his eyes on Meredith. He grinned and turned, heading swiftly back toward the kitchen, his arms swaying and his head held high.

"I DON'T KNOW what you were thinking back there, Meredith, but it certainly was the highlight of the evening," Katrina said as they pulled away in Henry's car.

Meredith was sitting in the backseat with her hands folded in her lap, staring out the window. She was strangely at ease with having challenged Chef Thayer. Somehow he seemed to invite confrontation. Also, his unsubtle probing for flattery nudged at something sore inside her, but she didn't know what, or why.

"Remind me not to take you to another nice restaurant, Meredith," Henry called playfully over his shoulder at her. "I shudder to think what they'll do to our food."

"Sorry," Meredith said, and let a closed-lipped grin slide across her face. "I don't know what came over me."

"Poor Chef Thayer didn't have a chance when you walked in the door," said Katrina. "I think until you're feeling better, we should keep you away from anyone who might piss you off—except for Nancy," she added.

Tara was looking at Meredith, but she didn't say anything.

Back at Henry's house, the four of them hugged all the way around and parted ways. Meredith and Tara drove home in silence, both deep in thought.

As they approached Meredith's house, Meredith looked around to make sure none of her neighbors were outside. With a silent curse she noticed that they all were collected together on Jodi and Mitch's porch, holding beers and lounging on chairs. As she slowed to pull into her driveway, they appeared to stop talking. Wes was leaning back with his feet up on a small table in front of him. His eyes followed her car for a moment or two, then turned up to the sky as he swigged his beer.

Meredith turned off the car and sat still for a moment.

"I'm really sorry you're going through this," Tara said. "It sucks."

Meredith nodded, her tears gathering a strength she herself did not feel. "Yes, it does."

"I hate that they're being so mean to you."

Meredith shrugged. "They've known him a long time, I guess. How would I react if somebody hurt you?"

"It's not the same. Wes didn't give you a choice."

They sat in silence, Meredith staring straight ahead.

Tara put her hand on Meredith's. "Hey," she said, moving her head to the side to force Meredith to look at her.

Meredith turned toward Tara.

"Screw them," Tara told her, tossing her head back to indicate the neighbors next door. "They don't know. They don't matter."

Meredith's mind was in turmoil. She didn't want to care, but she did. She knew what Tara was saying was true, but she was feeling vulnerable.

"I'm so tired," she said, and leaned her head back against the seat. "When will it be easy?"

Tara continued holding Meredith's hand in silence.

"I miss Wes. But I'm mad at him, too. How does that make sense?"

"Honey, it's normal to be mad at someone you love. You wouldn't be mad at him if you didn't care about him."

"I hate that he's right there but that I can't talk to him."

"I know. Soon you'll be able to, when it all blows over."

"I feel like I need to move. Why am I always running away?"

"One day you'll find your home, and you won't feel the need anymore. I just know it."

Meredith swallowed hard and closed her eyes. Suddenly she opened them and looked at Tara. "Do I bring this on myself somehow?"

"Of course not."

"You've been settled happily for almost ten years."

"I got lucky."

Meredith stared at her thoughtfully. Then she squeezed her hand. "All right," she said. "Let's get this over with."

Meredith and Tara climbed out of the car and shut the doors. They walked toward the house, arm in arm, without looking back. Tara stood behind Meredith as Meredith unlocked and opened her front door. Then they walked inside and shut the door behind them, blocking out the outside world until morning.

MEREDITH AND TARA decided to see a movie Saturday afternoon. Meredith had planned for them to spend a quiet day at the house, but Tara had insisted on their getting out.

"I don't know what I'd ever do without you, Tara," Meredith said. "You've been there for me so many times."

"I love you," Tara answered. "And I know you'd do the same for me."

They enjoyed the movie and a slice of pizza after, hanging out like they used to when they were in high school.

"The only thing missing is a prank call," Tara said.

"Call Vince," Meredith told her.

Tara took out her phone and demanded that Meredith give her Vince's number. She called him, leaving a sultry voicemail telling him she couldn't wait to see him that night while she was in town and that she'd meet him at the place they had agreed on.

She and Meredith erupted with laughter at the image of Vince frantically trying to figure out who he was supposed to see that night.

"I feel sort of bad about that," Meredith said, laughing through her tears.

"It serves him right," Tara said. "Maybe it wouldn't be so funny if there weren't so many women it could be."

When they arrived home, Meredith saw that Wes was outside pulling weeds out of his lawn. They sat in the driveway for a few moments, Meredith deep in thought.

She came to a decision.

"You go ahead inside," she said, handing Tara her keys. "I'll be right there."

Tara looked at her. "Are you sure you're ready for this?"

"No, but I have to do it."

They climbed out of the car. Tara headed up toward the house while Meredith stepped off the sidewalk and into the street toward Wes's house.

He looked up as she approached. He stared at her for a moment, then returned his attention to the weeds. Meredith was frightened, unsure of what was going to happen, but she kept moving; it was too late now.

As she stepped onto his lawn, he straightened, rubbing his hands together to sweep off the dirt. He looked at her, his jaw tight.

She stopped several feet away from him. "Hi," she said quietly.

"Hi," he replied, and bent over to drop a stray weed onto the pile.

They stood for a few moments in awkward silence, both looking at the ground.

"How are you?" she asked.

He looked at her again. "I'm all right."

They passed more time in silence.

"You?"

"I'm okay."

They stood there, loaded with questions and exclamations, neither knowing how to express them.

"Wes, I just wanted to tell you that—"

"Look, Meredith, you don't have to do this," he interrupted.

Meredith stared at him. "I don't have to do what?"

"You don't have to come over here and try to make nice with me. I'll be fine."

"But—"

"And I don't hate you," he added with a cheerless grin that did not reach his eyes, making his expression dark, almost ominous. "I know you did what you thought you had to do."

Her heart melted, and she frowned. "I did."

"I can't say I agree with you, but you always did have strong opinions."

"It isn't about strong opinions. It's—"

"Listen, Meredith," he said, holding his hands out to stop her. "Don't take this the wrong way, but I'm not in the mood to rehash everything with you right now. Was there anything you wanted?"

Meredith's chest had begun heaving as she felt her heart beat faster. She knew she had only minutes before the tears would start. "No," she replied, her voice shaky. "I just wanted to make sure you're okay."

"I'm okay. Thanks for checking on me."

She watched him. He looked as cool and calm as ever, his shoulders squared and his hands on his hips, his movements unhurried and smooth. But he was avoiding eye contact, and his foot was pounding lightly at an invisible something on the ground.

More time had passed than she had thought, and she felt his eyes on her. She met his gaze. He was looking at her expectantly.

"Was there anything else?"

Meredith wanted to tell him that she missed him, that she had found a restaurant he would like, that she had a lot of papers to grade and couldn't wait to snuggle with him in bed while she graded them, and did he need to borrow a book again? She felt the emotion seeping onto her face and knew he must be able to read her mind. When she looked at him, his expression had softened, and with horror Meredith realized that he was hoping she was going to tell him she wanted him back, that she had made a mistake. His eyes had become alert, and he had ceased the movement of his foot.

Meredith knew then that she had made a mistake in talking to him, that not enough time had passed and that it had been unfair of her to expect him to hold a conversation with her at this point —she couldn't even hold one with him, and the decision to split had been hers.

"No," she said, and lifted her hand in a gesture of goodbye. "That was all."

She turned and walked away toward her house, not looking back. She didn't want to see the look on his face, nor did she want him to see the agony on hers.

∾

TARA DID NOT MAKE Meredith go out that night. The two friends ordered Chinese food and awaited the delivery in their pajamas, each snuggled under a blanket in the family room, watching mindless television. It was exactly the kind of evening Meredith needed. Tara always seemed to know how to make her feel better.

The next day Tara hugged her goodbye. Meredith said she was due for a visit and that she couldn't wait to see the girls and Tom. In the meantime, she told Tara to tell the girls that Aunt Merry sent her love and that she missed them. She waved goodbye as Tara pulled away, leaving her on her own.

CHAPTER TWO

SHANE

*M*onday during lunch, Meredith and Katrina were sitting at a table in the faculty room, awaiting Henry. They were engaged in light chatter when he appeared in the doorway. He strode to their table with more spring in his step than usual and took his seat next to Meredith.

"Good afternoon, ladies." He folded his hands on the table and turned to Meredith. "I received a very interesting phone call this weekend," he told her.

"Oh?" Meredith said, unpacking her lunch.

"Yes. Would you care to guess whom it was from?"

Meredith sat still and thought for a moment, but no one came to mind.

"I'll give you a hint. Chef Shane Thayer."

Meredith dropped her bag on the table.

"What? Why was he—"

"He wanted to know how he could get in touch with you."

Out of the corner of her eye, Meredith saw Katrina's jaw drop open. Henry was still watching her, a grin spread across his face.

Meredith stammered, not knowing where to begin. "How did he even know how to get in touch with you?"

"He checked my reservation."

Meredith was silent as she considered what Henry was telling her.

Henry said, "I told him I didn't want to take it upon myself to hand out your number to strangers but that I'd be happy to take his and ask you to call him." At this point he dove into his brief-case, emerging with a piece of paper marked by a phone number written in Henry's neat hand. The name "Chef Shane Thayer" was printed above. Henry placed the paper firmly in front of Meredith.

She stared at it, dumbfounded.

"You must have made quite an impression on him if he went to all that trouble," Henry told her. "It looks like Chef Thayer enjoyed your not so friendly banter."

"What should I do?" Meredith asked desperately. "I don't even know the man! I just broke up with Wes two weeks ago. What kind of a person checks a reservation list to find the number of the friend of someone he wants to talk to?"

Scott turned in his seat and leaned over the back of his chair. He was sitting at a table across the room, having separated himself from the others so he could grade his papers in peace. "I say call him," he said. "How many chances do you get to date a famous chef?"

"I agree," said Katrina. "It can't hurt."

Meredith turned back to Henry.

"Of course I'm with the others," he said. "If nothing else, you know you'll get a good meal out of it."

MEREDITH WENT through the week mechanically, teaching her classes and grading her papers, meeting with Scott and the drama students in preparation for the play. The script had been written. Meredith and Scott were finishing up the editing, and the actors were already beginning to memorize lines. Meredith and Scott's role would decrease as soon as the editing was complete.

The weather was turning warmer now, and with dread Meredith noticed that she was seeing much more of her neighbors as they tended to their gardens and played outside with their children. She and Wes tried to avoid each other as much as possible but, as neighbors will, they encountered each other frequently, before and after work and as they picked up their mail and newspapers. They had exchanged brief, awkward waves and expressions of acknowledgement but had not spoken since Meredith's attempt the previous weekend.

However, Meredith did indulge in attempting to spy on him from her living room window. She was not proud of this. But her heart lurched with painful longing every time she saw him, and she needed a way to observe him in secrecy. She felt pathetic and sneaky, but she comforted herself with the thought that more than likely he was doing the same to her.

She had not yet returned Chef Thayer's phone call. She didn't know quite how to feel about it. She couldn't imagine why he would want to speak to her after the way she had challenged him at his restaurant. She knew she had been rude and confrontational, and she felt a pang of guilt when she thought about it. She was in no way ready to begin another relationship, especially with a man she didn't even like. There really was no reason for her to call him back.

Yet Thursday evening she found herself doing just that, for reasons she could not explain. As she withdrew the paper from her work bag and shakily dialed the phone number Henry had written on it, the only conclusion she could come to was that she was bored.

She got his voicemail and was going to hang up but at the last second decided to leave him a terse message, telling him who she was and that Henry had given her his number. She had no sooner put her phone on the counter, ready to forget him for the night, when he called her back.

She answered before she had a chance to grow nervous. "Hello," she said, trying to sound enthusiastic.

"Hi, Meredith. Sorry about that. I always screen all my calls."

Meredith rolled her eyes. She knew it wasn't unusual for people to screen their calls, but for some reason it sounded obnoxious coming from him.

"That's okay. Thanks for calling back."

"Thank *you* for calling back. I didn't know if you would. You certainly waited long enough. What's up—are you playing hard to get?"

Meredith was taken aback by his forwardness. "No," she said after a pause. "I've been busy."

"Busy doing what?"

Meredith did not know how to talk to Chef Thayer. He was acting as if they had known each other for years, as if they knew each other well enough for him to question her so. "Well, I'm a teacher, and I've been working," she said, a bit testily, "but also, to be honest, I wasn't sure whether I wanted to talk to you." She didn't know why she was always so inclined to be brutally upfront with him; hastily, before her words could sink in, she said, "I'm sorry. It has nothing to do with you. I just got out of a relationship."

"That works out well for me," he replied. "I was calling to find out if you'd go out with me Saturday night."

Meredith was bewildered. "Why?" she asked warily, because it was the first question that came to mind.

Now Chef Thayer paused, apparently equally dumbfounded. "Why? I don't know." He waited a few more seconds, and then said, "Because I think you're cute."

Meredith took a step backward. It seemed every time he opened his mouth he surprised her more and more. "Oh," she said, her mind swimming. She wasn't sure what to make of this response, but at least it made sense.

"So will you?"

Meredith shook her head. She knew she wasn't ready for a date; the thought to her seemed ridiculous. She didn't even know why she had called him to begin with. She wanted to get off the phone right away, to continue allowing herself to heal and to keep her promise to herself, to avoid pain. "I'm sorry," she said with genuine apology. "I just can't."

"I'll take you to any restaurant you want. I can get in anywhere. Where do you want to go?"

"The Spring House," she said without thinking, then instantly reprimanded herself for her boldness.

"Done. I'll pick you up at seven. What's your address?"

"I HAVE A DATE WITH CHEF THAYER," said Meredith as she sat down during lunch the next day. Already seated at the table were Henry, Katrina, and Scott. They looked up at her and froze, flabbergasted.

"Seriously?" said Katrina, a smile brightening her face. "When did this happen?"

"Last night. I called him back, finally. He asked me out. We're going to The Spring House tomorrow."

Henry whistled. "You didn't stand on ceremony when it came to getting him to take you there," he said, shaking his head. "Haven't you always wanted to go there?"

"He said he'd take me anywhere. I figured, why not?"

Scott was looking at her with a furrowed brow. "This isn't like you, Meredith. Is everything okay?"

Meredith turned to him. "What do you mean?"

"I don't know. You seem very blasé about the whole thing. Usually you take situations like this a bit more seriously."

"You're right, Scott," she said. "I don't know what's going on. I'm going through something. I don't know if it's good or bad."

"Well, whatever it is, keep it up," said Katrina. "It seems to be working for you."

"I don't know if I can help it," Meredith replied, taking a sip from her water bottle. "For some reason, Chef Thayer inspires me to say whatever is on my mind. I just can't bring myself to care what happens."

"Don't worry about it," said Henry. "Just have fun. And Meredith," he added, looking at her slyly.

"Yes?"

"I think you can start calling him Shane now."

MEREDITH HAD no trouble deciding what to wear on her date with Shane. It wasn't even a question. Saturday evening she strode into her bedroom and without hesitation slipped into the strappy red dress and tall black heels.

As she stared at herself in the mirror, she wondered what was going on with her. Scott had been right; she wasn't acting at all herself. Usually she was nervous and reserved around new men, playing safely by the rules. She had refused to wear this dress on her first date with Wes, and her feelings for him had been much stronger than her feelings for Shane. And she never would have spoken to Wes the way she had spoken to Shane, even toward the end of their relationship when they knew each other well and had already been through the fire. In addition, she realized that she knew nothing about Shane. She didn't know his history, his background, his likes or dislikes, his disposition, his temperament, or his age.

She decided not to worry about it, but to enjoy it, as Henry had advised. She was going to The Spring House, something she never thought she'd do. She was grateful for the distraction and hoped she'd have a nice time.

She was ready well before seven o'clock, but not because she had excitedly dressed early, as she had for her first date with Wes —it was because she had put very little time into her appearance. She spent a few moments tending to her hair, merely brushing it out and fluffing it up. She reapplied her makeup and wrapped a necklace around her neck, but otherwise she was unconcerned with fine details. At six-thirty she descended the staircase to wait in the kitchen with a cup of coffee.

Just after seven o'clock, her doorbell rang. She grabbed her purse and went to the door. When she swung it open, Shane was standing there, looking big and burly and ready for a night on the town. He was wearing a light gray suit with a pink shirt and polka-dotted tie. His hands were in his pockets, and the wide grin on his face made him appear cheerful and carefree. Meredith had to admit he looked stylish and handsome, and also fun. She began to grow excited to be going out with him.

"Hey," he said, looking her over. "Wow, you look great."

"Thanks," she said, smiling. "So do you. Are you ready to go?"

He backed up a few paces to give her room to exit and shut the door. As they were walking down the steps of her front porch, Meredith's excitement turned to distress when she saw Wes on the sidewalk between her house and the O'Reillys'; evidently he had just been over to see them and was heading home. It was the worst possible timing, and Meredith flushed, embarrassed and ashamed.

His pace slowed to a halt as he took in the sight of them, Meredith in the red dress he had so loved on her, headed toward Shane's sleek gray car. Meredith forced herself to look at him. He was staring at them, his lips tight and his eyes dark.

Shane was on the other side of his car, ready to climb into the driver's seat, but he paused when he saw that Meredith hadn't moved.

"What's up?" he asked, noticing Wes. Horrified, Meredith watched as he walked back around the car and held out his hand.

"Hi, I'm Shane Thayer," he said with unnecessary intensity.

His eyes fixed narrowly on Shane's face, Wes shook his hand. "I know who you are."

"Am I missing something?" Shane asked, looking back and forth between them.

"I'm sorry, Shane—this is Wes," Meredith said, extending her hand in Wes's direction. "Wes is my neighbor across the street."

At this description of her relationship with him, Wes's eyes blackened. "Yes," he said, his voice heavy with irony. "Meredith and I are neighbors."

Meredith braved a glance at him. He was watching her with a glower, and she flinched.

"Well, we'd better go," Shane said brightly. "We have a reservation." He turned to Wes. "We're going to The Spring House."

At Shane's words, Wes's face took on a look of pure contempt, and he clenched his jaw as he forced himself to hold his tongue.

"How nice," he managed to reply. He turned to Meredith. "Enjoy your date," he said, and stalked across the street.

IN THE CAR, Shane pulled the door shut and then faced Meredith. "What's with him?"

"Please just drive," she said in response.

Sniffling back tears, she turned her head toward the window to hide her face, now feeling guilty not only for hurting Wes but also for casting such awkwardness over her date with Shane. She pulled herself together and decided if Shane wanted to call off the date, if he thought she was ridiculous and never wanted to talk to her again, that would be fine by her.

But Shane did not seem put off or even surprised by her

display of emotion. He said, "Let me guess. That was the ex-boyfriend."

"Good guess."

Meredith sighed and sat up straight. "Can I be honest with you, Shane?"

"Okay."

"I'm kind of a mess," she said, and laughed. "Wes and I just broke up a few weeks ago. It's been hard, living across the street from him." She wiped her eyes. "You're meeting me at a difficult time."

"Hey, I don't care if you don't care. Messes don't bother me. I've been told I'm something of a mess myself."

She waited several moments before speaking again, then sighed. "I just hate to hurt him."

"Don't worry about your golden boy," Shane said offhandedly as he switched lanes. "He'll be fine."

Meredith stared at him, annoyed by how flippantly he could talk about something he knew nothing about. She smarted at the condescending tone with which he had referred to Wes.

"I'm sorry," Shane said, looking at her and noticing her dark expression. "Did something I say upset you?"

Meredith was having more and more trouble figuring out how to respond to him. "Please don't call him that."

"What should I call him?"

"Don't call him anything. Let's just change the subject."

They drove along in silence for some time. Meredith felt more and more awkward with each silent moment, fretting that he must think she was boring, an emotional wreck, and irritated with herself for caring.

"We seem a little short on conversation," she said, trying to make her voice bright.

"Hmm? What did you say?"

"I said we're a little short on conversation."

"I don't know what you mean."

She was growing impatient. "We don't seem to have anything to say." She faced him. "We haven't said anything in about ten minutes."

"Oh? I hadn't noticed."

Her face clouded with displeasure, and she faced forward, shaking her head.

Catching sight of her expression, he shot her a confused smile. "You're funny," he said.

Meredith now opened her mouth to say something but was at a loss. She couldn't decide if Shane was kidding with her or if he was completely clueless. She wasn't sure which she would prefer. She rubbed her face in her hands with exasperation.

Out of nowhere Shane screamed at the top of his lungs, his hands gripping the steering wheel; his eyes, which were large and alert under normal circumstances, looked positively spherical in profile.

Meredith screamed too, and grasped the sides of her seat with her hands, staring in front of her, expecting at any moment to see a truck or a bus slam into their car. When nothing happened, she turned to him, bewildered.

"Just lightening the mood," he said, his expression calm once again.

Meredith watched him with caution for a moment or two, concerned that she had trusted this person with her life. When it became apparent that he really did think he was lightening the mood, she faced forward once again and remained silent for the rest of the drive.

~

MEREDITH GLANCED around The Spring House. The interior was elegant but vibrant, just what she had expected. It was decorated to look like a conservatory, with black and white tiled floors and copious lush foliage in tall porcelain pots.

She and Shane had a spectacular table overlooking the garden in the back of the restaurant. They had walked right in, passing clusters of waiting guests, and approached the maitre d', who had taken one look at Shane and gestured with his fingers for him to follow. A bottle of champagne was waiting for them when they sat down.

Meredith turned to Shane and smiled. "Thank you for bringing me here. I've been wanting to come here for a long time."

"It's no problem," he said distractedly, fiddling with his phone. After a few moments, he looked up and returned her gaze, shoving his phone back into his pocket. He took her hands in his. "So," he said, "tell me all about yourself."

Meredith laughed. "What do you want to know?"

Shane's face was frozen into a wide-eyed smile. "Anything."

She shrugged. "Well, I'm a teacher. I'm originally from Philadelphia."

"You're from Philadelphia? Have you ever been to Sydney's?"

Meredith grinned. "As a matter of fact, I have. I was at the pilot of your show."

"That's funny," he said, slapping the table with both hands, but not laughing. "Not my shining moment. They canceled that show after four episodes, the bastards."

"What happened?"

"They said I wasn't likable enough."

At that moment, a waiter approached with appetizers Meredith had not been aware they had ordered. She didn't ask any questions and let Shane unceremoniously fill her plate.

"Since then I've been kind of lying low," he said. "I've had some minor appearances here and there, but mostly I'm just hanging out at the restaurant. My dad was the one who pushed me into the whole deal, but after it tanked he became nervous. Now he wants me to keep quiet so I don't spoil his reputation."

Meredith furrowed her brow, puzzled. "Why? Who is your father?"

He cocked his head and scrunched up his face. "You must not get out much," he said, twirling his fork around some pasta. "He's Senator Thayer. You didn't know that?"

"No!" she exclaimed with shock. Her heart was pounding. "I did not know that."

"Is that a problem?" he asked with a smirk.

"Not necessarily," she said, feeling the color seep into her face. "Just remind me not to tell my father."

Meredith recalled the biting editorial her father had written years ago about a contentious bill Maryland's Senator Thayer, then a representative, had tried to push through Congress. It had aroused strong feelings on both sides, and anyone in the political arena had been involved—including Meredith's father, who on the one hand had received enthusiastic praise, and on the other, death threats.

"Uh oh. Who's your father?"

"Harold Beck."

Shane leaned back in his chair and ran his hands through his hair, and laughed. "Are you freaking serious?" he asked, now leaning forward. "Christ, I remember when that editorial came out. What did my mother say about it?" He put his fingers to his chin and looked to the ceiling as he recalled the details. Then he returned his attention to his pasta and shrugged. "Ah, well—I can't remember the exact description, but I do believe it contained the words 'insane,' 'idiot,' and 'crap.'"

"Great," Meredith muttered, her shoulders falling. This foray out with Shane was beginning to look more and more unwise. She had accepted this date for superficial reasons—she had been grateful for the companionship and had jumped at the chance to be taken to this restaurant. She was ashamed enough as it was.

Her encounter with Wes had made her even more so. The fact that Shane's father was a man her own father so disliked was the final straw.

"I'm thinking this isn't meant to be," she said, her voice surprisingly bright, thankful that at least she had figured all this out early on. "Too many of the circumstances just aren't right."

"What are you talking about?" Shane asked as he poured her more champagne. "Your dad wrote an article about something my dad did. Because of that we can't have dinner?"

"I don't know, Shane," she said, already over him in her mind. "Between that and my recent breakup, I just think the timing is off. Plus, to be honest with you," she said, and favored him with a grin, "I only accepted this date to come to The Spring House." She figured she'd might as well be honest.

"I know that," he said through a mouth full of food. "I'm not stupid."

Meredith stared at him. "What?"

He swallowed and replied, "I don't need you to be in love with me right away. All I have to do is get you to go out with me. Then I work my magic." He held his arms out in front of himself while he did an odd little circular dance with his shoulders and chest.

Meredith said nothing, her eyes wide with bewilderment. Then she grinned, embarrassed, and blushed.

"Seriously, Meredith," he continued, more solemnly now. "We've been out only an hour, and already I know that you worry too much. Relax. I just want to take you out to dinner. We don't have to be best friends." He grinned. "We just have to have fun."

Warmed, Meredith couldn't help but return his smile. She watched him as he pummeled his mouth with appetizers, broke off a head of bread and then rubbed his hands together to brush off the crumbs.

Meredith attempted a new approach throughout the rest of dinner. She felt she had begun to understand Shane. She had to take him at face value and not expect him to adhere to subtle niceties of conversation or to indulge her in them. In return, he would require nothing of her other than her company, for her to be a positive presence with whom he could pass his Saturday night.

With this attitude, Meredith began to enjoy herself. It was nice not to have to worry so much about what she said, whether she was impressing him or offending him. She knew she couldn't possibly do either.

WHEN HE DROPPED her off at home, he parked in front of her house and said, without turning off the car, "Do you want me to walk you to your door?"

"No, that's okay," she said, and smiled, turning to him. "Thanks, though. And thanks for tonight. I had a nice time."

He was checking his phone. After a moment he replaced it in his pocket and turned to her. "You're welcome. Maybe I can take you out again next weekend."

Meredith wasn't sure how she felt about this. She didn't answer him for a moment, but he didn't seem to mind. Suddenly, before she understood what he was doing, he leaned in to kiss her; she turned her head to avoid him.

He backed away. "Well," he said. "Okay then."

"I'm sorry, Shane," she told him with a frown. "I'm just so mixed up right now that I don't know what to feel or what to do. I just need a little time." She paused. "I hope that's okay."

"Sure, it's fine," he said, with an amiable smile. "I get it. I can respect that." He patted her on top of the head instead. "How's that?"

She laughed. "That I think I can handle."

"So what time should I pick you up next Saturday? I'll take you somewhere really wild. I'll surprise you."

Meredith hesitated.

"It's just dinner, Meredith," he said.

She looked at him squarely. "Okay."

"Great. Pick you up at seven?"

"Sure," she said, and smiled. "Great."

She unbuckled her seatbelt and opened the door.

"Goodnight," she said.

"Goodnight."

She climbed out of the car and stood on the curb as he pulled away, waving as he drove off, then looked across the street toward Wes's house. There was a light on in the living room; every other window was dark. She wondered if he was watching her right now, and if so, what he was thinking. She turned and walked up to her front door and headed inside.

Once settled, she sat back and thought about the situation with Shane. Her one requirement for a man was that her relationship with him be easy, free of drama and heartache. With Shane, she didn't have to worry about conversation because he was unconcerned with formalities and etiquette. She didn't have to avoid being honest because he didn't seem to care about much of anything. She had promised herself that she would not involve herself with another man except for the company, that she wouldn't risk the pain involved with seeing another man she could fall in love with—she had no strong feelings for Shane, and yet they had a convenient common interest, which was food. And she didn't have to feel guilty about using him because he knew she was doing it, and he seemed content to let her. Add to that the fact that he evidently wasn't going to pressure her when it came to the physical aspect of the relationship, and Meredith could come to only one conclusion.

He was perfect.

MEREDITH HAD trouble falling asleep that night. As she lay in bed, on her back, her arms at her sides and her face pointed up at the ceiling, all she could think about was Wes. She closed her eyes and imagined him next to her, could almost feel his legs slinking through hers. She tingled when she recalled the way his hands had felt as they had roamed all over her, tenderly at first and then firmly, the way they positioned and guided her, patient but determined. She missed the way his voice turned low and insistent at night; in spite of her misgivings, she had found him irresistible when he was leading her, had found his confidence magnetizing. She missed the way his sandy hair felt between her fingers, the way his face felt in her hands, his lips soft as they parted with his hurried breaths.

She turned, frustrated, onto her side. Facing his side of the bed made her miss him more, however, and she sat up, feeling restless and depressed. She switched on the light and walked to the window, peering out from behind the curtains so she could observe the activity at Wes's house.

Now all the lights downstairs were off. Only his bedroom was lit. Meredith imagined him in his bedroom, wondered what he was doing, whether he was lying awake like she had been, whether he was thinking of her or trying to distract himself with a book or work.

Suddenly she had her answer. The curtain at his window opened from the middle, and before she knew it she was looking at Wes, who apparently had had the same idea she had, and was staring at her from across the street. Startled, she closed the curtain and stepped back. But then, on an impulse she could not control, she cautiously opened the curtain again, to see if he was still there. He was, but on noticing her he too was startled, and he pulled back just as she had. She waited for several minutes, but he did not reappear. Soon his bedroom light turned off. Meredith continued to stare at his window, imagining him in bed, wondering what he was wearing and how long it would take him to fall asleep. She knew he was thinking of her, and the thought made her yearn for him even more. Remembering that they had neglected to exchange the keys they had shared, she was tempted to let herself into his house. She closed her eyes and lifted her chin toward the ceiling as she imagined how good it would feel to be with him again, how good it would feel to alleviate his pain. Only when the tears came did she surrender, climbing back into bed and crying herself to sleep once more.

CHAPTER THREE

OBSERVATIONS

*S*unday was rainy and cold. Meredith let herself sleep in and then spent the morning indoors, catching up on her schoolwork while drifting in and out of reveries, trying to push off the gloom that had been weighing on her since her breakup with Wes almost a month before.

Without warning, she was struck by a powerful urge. She stood, slipped into her jacket, and walked next door to the O'Reillys' house.

She strode up the steps onto their porch and to their door, then rang the bell before she could stop herself. After a few moments, the door was opened by Mitch. He looked surprised to see her.

"Hi, Meredith," he said. "Jodi's not here."

"Oh," she replied, her face falling. "Do you know when she'll be back?"

"She took the boys to a play date. She'll be back in a few hours, I'd think."

"Okay. Thanks," she said, and smiled, preparing to leave.

Mitch returned her smile and began to shut the door. All of a sudden Meredith called him back.

"Mitch," she cried, extending her arm out to stop him.

He paused, opening the door wide again and looking at her expectantly.

"Um," she faltered, not knowing what to say. "Can I talk to you for a minute?"

He hesitated, then smiled weakly. "Sure," he said, stepping onto the porch and closing the door.

Meredith watched Mitch. He was tall and friendly-looking, with wavy brown hair and a kind expression. He was dressed casually in jeans and a black sweatshirt, and as he stood awkwardly before her Meredith decided that the only approach she could affect was that of honesty.

"Mitch," she said, "I hope you know that I never meant to hurt Wes. It was the last thing in the world I wanted to do."

Mitch frowned as he looked at her. He sighed, his entire body rising and falling with sorrow. His expression softened. "I know that," he said. "I know you'd never deliberately hurt him, or anyone."

Meredith's eyes were clouded by tears. She was so grateful to him for saying those words, for not assuming she was a horrible person, for at least trying to see the situation from her point of view.

"Thank you, Mitch," she said, trying to keep her voice steady. "I really appreciate that."

Mitch waited patiently for her to calm herself. They stood in tense silence for many moments before he spoke again.

"You know, Meredith," he said, not looking at her—his eyes were fixed on her feet, "you shouldn't blame us for being there for Wes. We've all known him a long time, since long before he and Claire divorced."

"I know that," Meredith said, growing annoyed. She had heard this comment several times and was well aware of the closeness the neighbors shared. "But it doesn't make him perfect."

Mitch was silent. He continued to avoid her gaze.

Meredith didn't know what else to say. It seemed pretty clear by now that she and the neighbors were at an impasse. She felt the loss but couldn't bring herself to grieve it. She was tired of grieving. She was just getting ready to thank Mitch and bid him goodbye when he spoke again.

"Did you have a date last night?"

Meredith looked at him, surprised by his boldness. Now he was looking at her, clearly uncomfortable but forcing himself to meet her gaze anyway, prepared to wait for an answer. Meredith was irritated. This was none of his business.

She was about to tell him as much when she abruptly changed her tactic. "Yes," she said. "Did Wes tell you that?"

"Yes. He said he ran into you as you were leaving."

"He did. He seemed pretty upset. I don't blame him. I'm sure I'd feel the same way if the situation were reversed."

"He thought it was a little soon for you to be dating," Mitch said, and Meredith knew that by telling her what Wes had said, he also was expressing his own opinion.

"You know, Mitch," Meredith responded, "I know it's soon. But I need something to take my mind off my problems. I'm hurting too, though nobody seems to remember that." All of a sudden she was crying again, though that hadn't been her intention. "All I was doing was sitting around missing Wes. And then Shane came along and became a distraction. I had to get out," she said as she wiped her tears with her sleeve. "It's nothing serious. Nothing like what I had with Wes." She sighed and rubbed her face in her hands. "I'm sorry. I just can't seem to stop crying."

Mitch was watching her. His expression was unreadable. Meredith gathered that he didn't know what to think or what to say. She felt a surge of sympathy for Mitch. It was obvious that he didn't want to be involved in this, that it was difficult for him to express his opinions and that he hated having to stand here with her and act as a diplomat, trying to decide what he should tell her and what he shouldn't. She knew he had no hard feelings against her but that there was no way he could extend his hand to her, given the circumstances. She understood all this and felt warmly toward him, appreciating his position and admiring him for being brave enough to take as much action as he had.

"If you wanted Wes back, I know he'd take you," Mitch murmured, and Meredith had the impression that he was not, in fact, authorized to say those words. Meredith felt instinctively that Wes had expressly told him not to, both to save face and to prevent her from going back to him for any reasons other than her own.

"I can't do that," Meredith said with a frown, shaking her head, "though I want to." She thought carefully about how to conclude her performance. Finally, she said, "I love Wes, and I want him to be happy. I think maybe one day he'll see this was for the best."

She straightened, smiled at Mitch, and walked down the steps and across the lawn to her own house. She knew Mitch would tell Wes everything she had said. She hoped her words would comfort him, even a little.

MEREDITH'S SCHOOL week was blessedly monotonous, except for one incident midway through that cast a grim cloud over the remaining days.

It was morning, and Meredith was looking forward to teaching her lively freshmen, who had become more confident and were participating with bright, thoughtful ideas. Meredith was proud of them. By now they were writing lucid, organized essays and were sharp, astute readers. Meredith had grown to love them all and eagerly awaited them, her copy of *To Kill a Mockingbird* in hand.

The door opened, and Meredith glanced upward. However,

instead of a freshman, Meredith's gaze landed on Nancy who, clipboard in hand, approached Meredith's desk with a stony smile.

"Hello, Meredith. I'll be observing your class today. Just pretend I'm not here."

"Okay," Meredith said, trying not to be nervous.

Her freshmen filtered in, their vibrant conversation ceasing as soon as their eyes fell on their stern principal. Meredith watched them, dismayed. She hoped they wouldn't be too intimidated for conversation today. When class started, she briefly addressed Nancy's presence, to allay their fears.

"Good morning, everyone," she said, her voice upbeat and casual. "As you've noticed, Mrs. Zales is here. She will be looking in on our class today. You've probably seen her observing other classes, as well. It's our job to just go about business as usual and continue our discussion." With that, she delved right in.

She was pleased with the session. The students warmed as soon as she opened the conversation, pointing to specific passages and choosing students to respond from the sea of many hands raised into the air. She felt the lesson was cohesive and that the students demonstrated their understanding. Meredith was impressed by the connections they made to other points in the book as well as to other works entirely, and she was delighted to be able to reference earlier lessons, thus tying together material learned throughout the year. When the bell rang, Meredith reminded them that their essays were due on Friday. With that, the students packed up and left, cheerful smiles on their faces.

When the last student had walked out and closed the door, Meredith turned to Nancy and smiled. Nancy was writing on her clipboard and said nothing for some time. Meredith mindlessly organized some papers on her desk while she waited.

Finally Nancy stood and took a few steps toward Meredith.

"I'm a little concerned about Mike Ellison," she said. "I wasn't sure he was getting what you were saying."

Meredith was taken aback. She thought for a moment. "I don't believe Mike answered any questions today."

"Exactly," Nancy said. "How will you know if your students are picking up on the lessons, if you aren't calling on them?"

Meredith's heart sank. She had been so proud of herself and her students and had felt sure that Nancy would have something positive to say, this time. Hiding her frustration, she said, "Well, he volunteers to answer questions all the time. No student speaks every day. I'm sure he'll speak up tomorrow, and if not, I'll call on him then."

"Why wait that long? Why not just take a moment before the lesson to allow each student to ask a question about the previous day's class?"

Meredith furrowed her eyebrows. "You want each student to ask a question at the beginning of every class?"

"Yes. Five minutes is all it should take. That way you know you're getting through to each student."

Meredith was livid. She felt she was diligent enough to discern which students were not contributing on a regular basis and to ensure, at her own discretion, that they were doing so. She also balked at the idea that she could individually question twenty students in five minutes. In order to do that, she would need nearly the entire period.

Nancy continued, "And while you're at it, I didn't hear any summary of the lesson. You should be taking a minute or two at the end of each class period to relay the point of the lesson, to make sure they understand how it ties together and relates to everything else you've done."

"You're right in that I did not take specific time at the end of class to do that, but we did that during the rest of the period. Actually, the students did it all on their own. I think that shows the point is being made."

"But they will remember most clearly what is said at the end of class. The last thing you told them was that their essays are due on Friday, and even that was an afterthought. Frankly, I don't feel that you're organizing your time as efficiently as you could."

Meredith wanted to tell Nancy that she had been teaching for over ten years and had never been told this, that the success of her students suggested otherwise and that it was easy for Nancy to come in and observe one lesson, and make a snap judgment based on one student's behavior over the course of an hour.

"I'll observe another class next week to make sure these changes are being implemented," Nancy said on her way out the door. "Thank you, Meredith," she added, and left.

During lunch, Meredith asked Katrina and Scott whether Nancy had visited their classes and made similar suggestions. They looked at her with confusion and told her that, yes, Nancy had been in to observe but that she hadn't said anything like that, even though neither of them ever began class with a question and answer period, as Nancy had requested of Meredith. Meredith shook her head. She didn't know why Nancy insisted on targeting her like this, nor how much longer she could tolerate it.

SATURDAY NIGHT MEREDITH prepared for her second date with Shane. When her doorbell rang, she was just descending the staircase and went right to the door. He was dressed fashionably in a black suit with a black shirt, and no tie.

"The black is nice," she said with a smile as she picked up her purse. "You wear it well."

"Thanks. I like black. It makes me feel fast." Here he suddenly turned sideways, spreading his legs and bending his knees, and threw out his arms, one in back and one in front.

Meredith laughed. "It must be working. I almost didn't see that."

She followed him down the front steps and toward his car,

looking warily around her. She was relieved to find that none of her neighbors were outside.

In the car, Shane said, "You-know-who isn't out today. He must be steering clear."

"I'm sure he's not deliberately keeping away," Meredith replied. "He's probably just inside."

Meredith glumly watched Wes's house as they pulled away. Shane was unlike Wes in every way, and part of her enjoyed his goofiness—but she missed Wes's dry, smart wit. She was hit again by how wrong Shane was for her. She put the thought out of her mind, telling herself to just relax and have fun.

"I never even asked where you live," she said as Shane drove toward downtown Washington.

"I live in Maryland."

"Are you just over the border?"

"No. I live west of Washington, toward Frederick."

She turned to him, surprised. "That's a long drive. You're really going to a lot of trouble to pick me up."

"It's no trouble," he said. "I like to get out."

"Do you work very long hours?"

"My hours are brutal during the week, but I don't work Saturdays or Sundays."

Meredith sat still for a moment, trying to come up with something else to say. She couldn't, and began to feel the familiar awkwardness. She was just thinking that the length of the silence had passed the point of absurdity when he turned to her with a smile.

"By the way, I never told you how pretty you look. I was too busy being fast."

"You were so fast you didn't even notice," she said, laughing. "Thanks, though. That's nice."

His compliment had lightened the mood but had done nothing to improve the conversation. Meredith felt it incumbent on herself to try again.

"Have you had many television appearances?"

"Not really. I judged a couple of contests here and there, but it wasn't anything spectacular. Nothing that would propel me into the limelight, anyway."

"Is that what you want?"

"I don't know. It could be fun, but I don't think I want all the responsibility. The show was hard. I can't say I was broken up when it was over."

Meredith had a question, but she wasn't sure if it would offend him. "How did you end up with the show at all? I mean, if—"

"It's all about who you know, Meredith," he interrupted, and suddenly his eyes turned dark.

Uncomfortable now, Meredith decided to change the subject.

"You drive a long way to work every day."

"Yeah. The commute is a drag, but that's where my house is."

Meredith didn't ask any more questions. She was getting the feeling there was more to the situation than he was willing to tell her, and she didn't want to push him.

"Well," she said, "if we go out again, I'd be happy to meet you somewhere closer to where you live. You don't have to pick me up every time if you're driving such a long way."

He looked at her, his expression softening. Then he looked back at the road. "Nah, don't worry about it."

Meredith leaned back in her seat and was silent, deciding not to speak again unless spoken to first.

SHANE TOOK her to another fancy restaurant of which she had never expected to see the inside. Once again they walked right in and were directed to one of the best tables in the room, this time just next to a large fireplace that at this time of year was filled with glowing candles.

Meredith learned a little more about him during the course of their conversation, where he had attended college and how he had become involved with food. She gathered that while he had natural skill and genuine interest in cooking, it was just one of many possible career choices he could have made. She didn't know if this made him talented or fickle, or both. He seemed to enjoy his career but didn't appear passionate about it, not even as passionate as she was about her own cooking. He appeared to lose interest when she told him about her own creations, asking his advice and earnestly trying to engage him in conversation about the one common interest they held. She wasn't sure if his apathy suggested that he didn't think she was qualified to talk to him about it, or if he simply didn't care—and she didn't know him well enough to make an educated guess. He continued to be a mystery to her, and she was beginning to think she'd never be able to crack it. As happy as she had been to find a companion to distract her, she was dismayed. She didn't think even she could handle this little connection.

She was prepared to write off the evening and politely decline further invitations, if any further invitations were to be forthcoming. Then he surprised her.

"Hey, listen," he said after their plates had been cleared. "You're a really nice person. I'm glad I asked you out." He smiled, then laughed. "I don't think I've ever been out with a nice person before."

Meredith was touched. "Thank you. That was a sweet thing to say."

"To be honest, you make me a little nervous," he said then. "I don't know how to act around you. I'm used to dating a very different kind of woman."

"What kind of woman is that?"

"I don't want to use language that will offend your delicate ears," he said playfully, patting her hand. "Let's just say they're not like you."

"How do you know?"

He stared at her and grinned. "I guess I don't. Are you telling me you're not such a nice girl after all?"

"Would that make you happy or sad?"

He furrowed his brow, then laughed again. "I really don't know."

"Well," she said, "I appreciate your sentiment, but please don't be nervous around me. I'm about as non-threatening as it gets." She smiled; he had begun to endear himself to her. "Actually, I've been thinking that I don't know how to behave around you either. You seem so nonchalant, but somehow I'm thinking you run very deep."

He shrugged. "I'm just a guy." He pulled out his phone and looked at the screen, frowning.

Meredith waited for him to say more, but he didn't.

"Have you ever made pâté en croûte?" she asked him, randomly; she didn't want them to lose their momentum, and it was the first question that came to mind. And anyway, she was curious.

"Pâté en croûte?" he asked, absentmindedly, punching something into his phone. "Yeah, of course."

She nodded, looking around the room, waiting for the return of his attention. "Is it hard?"

"Not if you know what you're doing."

They managed to chat with a bit more enthusiasm on the way home than they had on the way out, though Meredith still felt pressured to jumpstart the conversation more than once. As they pulled in front of her house, Shane turned to her.

"So what do you say? Do you want to go out again tomorrow?"

Meredith was puzzled. She didn't know what Shane saw in her. Other than his lovely comment in the restaurant, he hadn't demonstrated that he had any interest in anything about her. She had noticed that he never asked her any questions; she frequently inquired about his life, but he had yet to ask for even one detail about her own. Even when the conversation turned to her, he managed to work it back to himself. She wondered with confusion why he wanted to see her again, other than the fact that he thought she was "pretty" and "nice."

She wanted to ask him all this, but she didn't want to put an unnecessary strain on whatever it was they were involved in—she hesitated to call it a relationship. She decided she'd go out with him one more time. She would make her decision after that.

"Sure. Same time?"

"No, I have plans tomorrow night. How about lunch? Pick you up at noon?"

"Okay," she said, eager for the change.

"Dress casually. See you then."

She climbed out of the car and stood on the sidewalk as he pulled away. She waved as he drove down the street, then turned and went inside.

SUNDAY AFTERNOON she slipped into a pair of jeans and a white shirt, topping it with a beige jacket and checking herself in the mirror with just enough time before the doorbell rang. She groaned inwardly when, walking with Shane down the steps, she saw Wes sitting on his front porch with a newspaper. His feet resting on the table, he appeared absorbed in his reading; he was pretending not to see them, and Meredith was embarrassed but relieved when he did not make eye contact.

Eager to escape as quickly as possible, she had just opened the door of Shane's car when Shane, on his way to the driver's side, startled her by calling across the street to Wes.

"Hey man, don't wait up."

Meredith froze. Her eyes darted to Wes. He was sitting still, glaring at Shane. Evidently deciding to ignore this taunt, he said nothing and turned back to his paper.

Shane went on.

"Nah, I'm just messing with you. I'll try to have her home at a reasonable hour. Okay?"

"Shane," Meredith muttered under her breath, with mounting horror. "What are you doing?"

Wes's eyes had narrowed. He was silent for a few tense moments.

"You do that," he called back.

Shane held up his hands. "No hard feelings, right? We're cool, right?"

Wes lowered his paper, and a dark grin crossed his face. "Yes, Shane," he said. "We're cool." He lifted the paper and held it close to his face, shaking his head.

"Awesome," said Shane, and opened his door. "I'm glad you don't resent me for horning in on your territory." He fell into his seat and shut the door.

Meredith didn't know what to do. She wanted to address Wes but was too infuriated not to confront Shane. Glancing once at Wes, who was watching her from the porch, she opened the passenger's side door and stuck her head inside the car.

"What the hell was that about?"

"What do you mean?"

"You know what I mean! You were deliberately baiting Wes. What were you thinking?"

"All right, I admit it. I don't know what came over me. I'm sorry." He looked at her earnestly, though Meredith couldn't tell if he was sincere or just a very good actor. "It won't happen again."

"You're damn right it won't happen again. I'm not going out with you today or any other day. That was malicious and cruel, and I can't tolerate it. Goodbye, Shane," she said, and straightened to shut the door.

"No, Meredith, wait," he said, reaching for her. "Really, I'm sorry. That was mean of me, I know. I'll go over there right now and apologize, if you think it would help."

Meredith sighed and leaned into the car once more. "I doubt

it would help. I'm sure he wants to forget all about it. I know I do."

"Please don't go. Look, I'm nervous, okay? Sometimes I do stupid things when I'm nervous. Don't go just because I made one mistake." His eyebrows rose, asking for her agreement.

Meredith believed that this one act had said more about him than any words he had spoken thus far, that any person who could treat someone else with such disrespect was not a person she wanted to have anything to do with. She shook her head.

"I'm sorry, Shane. Even I'm not that desperate," she said, and slammed the door.

He waited only a moment before driving off. Meredith looked toward Wes's house; he was nowhere to be seen. Fuming, she walked back into her house, feeling sad and lonely. As ambivalent as she had been about Shane, she had looked forward to having something fun to do and to not knowing what was going to happen next. Now she had nothing to look forward to but loneliness and grief, once again. She flopped onto the living room couch, resolving to spend the day grading papers and eating ice cream.

Her phone vibrated. She removed it from her purse and looked at it. She had a text from Shane:

"I'm sorry. I'm an idiot. Call me if you change your mind."

She texted back:

"Don't text while you're driving. You might kill someone."

MEREDITH SAT on the couch for a long time, thinking. Her legs were crossed, and her arms were folded over her chest. She was trying to resist an urge that was becoming more and more difficult to suppress. At some point, she didn't know when, she understood that she was no longer trying to suppress the urge, only to gather the strength to gratify it.

Abruptly she stood and walked with even steps to her front door. She marched down the stairs of her porch and across the street to Wes's house. She strode up the steps and to his front door, then rang the bell firmly, deliberately not thinking, not giving herself time to talk herself out of it.

She was going to apologize to Wes for Shane's cruel behavior. Then, she was going to beg him to take her back.

She knew it was the right thing to do. She didn't know why it had taken her this long to figure it out.

As she waited for him to answer the door, she berated herself for having been so stupid. Here in this house was a decent, generous, successful, charming, loving, handsome man who had proposed to her twice and bought her a house, so eager was he to spend the rest of his life with her. She genuinely loved him and had thought of him nearly every second since they had separated. She wondered how foolish she must be to have rejected him, twice. Each second she waited on his porch was another second of torment before she could tell him she wanted to marry him right then and there, the sooner the better.

The door swung open, and there he was, looking shocked beyond belief to see her.

"Hi," he said, his eyebrows forked downward with confusion.

"Hi," she replied, breathless. "Can I come in?"

"Sure," he said, and stepped back to let her through.

Being in his house again, Meredith was overwhelmed with memories. As she looked around she remembered the joyful times they had spent here, how it had become like her home, too. She turned to him with tears in her eyes.

"Wes, I'm so sorry. That was horrible of Shane. I told him so and sent him off."

Wes was standing still, his arms down at his sides and his eyes fixed on her. In his stylish slacks and polo shirt, he looked like the dapper but easygoing Wes she loved, and she was just waiting for him to respond so she could wrap her arms around him and eliminate the last month of pain, resuming where they had left off.

"Thank you," he said. His voice was low and even, and remarkably calm. "I have to admit that I was wondering what you were doing with that clown. But I'm pleased to see you've come to your senses."

Meredith paused, vaguely irritated by his tone. After a moment, during which she dismissed her annoyance as the product of oversensitivity, she continued: "I feel terrible for having hurt you. It wasn't my intention. I know what you must think," she said, her voice catching, "that my dating so soon must be an indication of my feelings for you, or lack thereof. But that just isn't true. Quite the opposite, in fact." She took a deep breath and prepared to get to the point.

But she didn't have time. Before she could continue, Wes folded his arms, and his face assumed a thoughtful frown. "You know, Meredith, I'm not going to stand here and try to convince you that it doesn't bother me. However, I think I understand why you would put yourself out there again right away, and I don't hold it against you." He inhaled deeply, and his expression turned more serious. "But I don't want you seeing Shane Thayer anymore. If you feel strongly that you can't make it work between us, that's something we'll both have to deal with, and if that's the case then I have to accept that you're going to go out with other men. But not Shane Thayer. I don't like him. He's all wrong for you, Meredith, and even if I have to live my life without you, I can't tolerate the idea of you spending your life with someone like him."

Meredith opened her eyes wide, aghast. Her lips parted as she prepared to say something, but she didn't know what to say. As his words sank in, she began to grow resentful.

"First of all," she said, her voice quiet and controlled, holding her hands up to slow him down, "what do you mean, if I can't make it work between us?"

"Just what I said. You're the one who wants this split, Meredith, not me. If it were up to me, we'd be married by now and living in Wellbourne. You're the one who wasn't happy."

"So what you're saying is that if I wasn't happy, that was my fault?"

"Well, look at the facts!" He threw his hands in the air and then down to his sides, where he shoved them into his pockets. "I would have given you the perfect life. You never would have wanted for anything. I could not have tried any harder to make you happy. I was offering you everything any person in their right mind could dream of, and if you still were unsatisfied, well, there really wasn't anything more I could have done."

Meredith could not believe what she was hearing. Overwhelmed, she closed her eyes and shook her head. There was way too much to say about that, and it was beside the point. She decided to put it aside and come back to it later. Opening her eyes, she said, "You don't have the right to tell me whether I can see Shane or not, whatever your opinion of him. I'm the only one who decides who is right for me and wrong for me. You're going to have to 'tolerate' it whether you like it or not."

Wes laughed grimly. "Forgive me if I don't put much stock into your ability to determine who is right and who is wrong for you. You understand where I'm coming from, of course."

Meredith wondered if he possibly could be more condescending. She knew he was hurting, but he was dangerously skirting the boundary between pain and malice. "It's no longer any of your business," she said, her voice shaking. "You have no control over me anymore. In fact maybe if you had given up a little control when we were together, we wouldn't be standing here arguing, and Shane wouldn't be in the picture to begin with."

"I'm just calling it as I see it. Maybe you're not seeing it objectively, but to me it's perfectly clear. Shane Thayer is a punk, and you should have nothing to do with him. I'm telling you, Meredith. I don't want you to see him again. If you ever had any feelings for me at all, you won't." He crossed his arms in a gesture of challenge, daring her to defy him.

Meredith took a couple of steps backward, devastated. She had come over here overflowing with joy and excitement. She was now looking at being left alone for the second time that day. As she stared at Wes, she understood that she had been right, that he would never change, and that she would never be able to impart to him that her inability to find happiness in his dream was not a failure on her part, but on his.

Feeling as if she could not be any more depressed, she turned away from him and headed toward the door. Just before leaving, she faced him once more, with the purpose of informing him that she had in fact gone over there to take him back, that had he just controlled himself for five minutes they would have ended up happily ever after, that he had only himself to blame for their current misery.

He was standing there, looking sadder and more vulnerable now that she had taken so many steps away from him. He was unfolding his arms and slowly bringing them once again to his sides; his face wore a pathetic frown. Suddenly she didn't have the heart to tell him that she had been planning to take him back. She couldn't hurt him that way. As indignant with him as she was for having lashed out at her in anger, she couldn't bring herself to do the same to him.

"Goodbye, Wes," she said dejectedly as she opened the door to leave. "I love you," she told him then, unable to stop herself, as she closed it on her way out.

"Hey, babe. What's up? Are you still mad at me?"

"Yes," Meredith said, "but I'm willing to put it behind me."

"Awesome," Shane responded, and there was some interference on the other end as he either switched ears or bumped into somebody. "So does that mean you'll give me another chance?"

"If you promise to stop being a jackass."

"I can't promise that. But I can promise to stop yelling to your neighbor from across the street."

Meredith closed her eyes in surrender. She was sitting on a stool at the kitchen island, and she leaned her elbow on the countertop and rested her head in her hand, shaking it slowly. "All right," she said. "It's a deal." She was about to hang up the phone, but suddenly she decided she was through with games and was going to ask him the question that had been burning in her mind since the night before. "Shane," she said, sitting a little straighter, "just tell me one thing."

"What's that?"

"Why do you even care?"

There was silence on the other end. "Care about what?"

"Why do you even want to see me again?"

"Do I need a reason?"

"Yes."

Meredith waited while he considered. Finally, he said, "I already told you. You're nice. It's a change of pace for me. I'm ready to be nice. I'm ready to slow down and start taking life seriously." There was a short pause here, during which Meredith imagined him putting his hands in the air and smiling in his playful way. "I might as well partner up with someone who can show me how."

Meredith's forehead rose with interest. It was not the answer she had been expecting. It made her feel better about forgiving him; it was a reminder that one mistake does not always define us, that many times, the hurt people cause is rooted in hurt deep within themselves. It suited her just fine, and she told him to call her the next day. She hung up the phone, satisfied.

She sat for several minutes, mindlessly twirling her phone in her fingers, before getting up. She didn't know what had driven her to Shane. Her journey had been a long and arduous one, fraught with pain and challenges but also with happiness and laughter. She didn't know how she had ended up here, but she felt somehow that it was the end of the road. She was exhausted. She could not imagine starting over yet again, planning yet another life, always wondering what was around the next corner. For some inexplicable reason she believed she and Shane were meant to be, that what she was looking at right now was the conclusion to her story, that she would finally have some peace. The unknown was killing her. She felt that the universe had thrown her and Shane together for a reason; why else would they have been crossing paths since the beginning of her journey? They did not love each other and likely never would; however, each served a purpose to the other, and she sensed that they could have a mutual understanding that would work equally well for both of them. She knew it was quite early to be thinking about this. But she also believed she had very good instincts, and her instincts were telling her that there wouldn't be anyone new after Shane.

CHAPTER FOUR

MARIBEL

*M*eredith acknowledged that, somewhere in the deep recesses of her mind, she was dating Shane to teach Wes that he couldn't control her. She resented his misguided belief that he had some say over what she did now, and she wanted him to know that she was capable of making her own decisions and would do so regardless of his opinions.

But mostly she was nervous about the two men meeting again. She didn't want to inflict any more pain on Wes.

Shane had called her on Monday, as she had requested, and they had arranged for him to pick her up the following Saturday night. Meredith was looking forward to the date but not with the same kind of lovelorn delirium with which she had looked forward to dates in the past. She enjoyed Shane's company but was more eager to get out of the house than to see him. She told herself that it wasn't fair to Shane. Having decided to give him another chance, she was content to let the relationship take its course. But she had to at least like him. She decided that if her feelings for him didn't start improving soon, she would have to stop seeing him.

Saturday evening she had been waiting for about ten minutes

after seven o'clock when she decided to peer outside to see if his car was approaching. She was startled to discover that it was parked in front of her house. With horror she saw that Shane was standing on the sidewalk in front of Wes's house. He and Wes appeared to be deep in conversation.

She grabbed her purse and keys and stalked out the front door, then crossed the street with wide, quick steps. Shane's back was to her. He was standing casually, one foot on the street and the other on the curb. His hands were in his pockets, and his broad back was straight and tall. His thick frame looked impressive, almost threatening, in his gray suit, white shirt, and yellow tie. Meredith's eyes shifted to Wes. He was wearing jeans and a t-shirt, which was covered by an unbuttoned plaid collared shirt, the sleeves rolled up to his elbows. His arms were folded over his chest, and his weight rested on one hip. As Shane spoke, Wes was watching him with an interested expression. Meredith thought it seemed to carry with it a mixture of curiosity, disgust, and amusement.

At her approach, Wes turned his head to look at her. His expression lightened slightly; somehow he gave the impression of smiling without actually doing so. His face seemed tinged with bewildered pleasure, almost as if Shane was entertaining him. Meredith wasn't sure if she liked this change or not. She was glad Wes no longer appeared angry, but there was something sinister about his appearance, almost as if he knew something she didn't.

When he noticed that Wes was no longer watching him, Shane turned in the direction of his gaze. As opposed to Wes's almost wickedly pleased expression, Shane's face was serious and intense, and the contrast between them unnerved Meredith. She had no idea what was going on, but something about the situation made her uneasy.

"Hi," she said, breathless from having walked so quickly. She turned to Shane. "What are you doing? I've been waiting for you for ten minutes."

"Sorry," he replied, smiling amiably. "I saw your neighbor outside and just thought I'd say hello before picking you up. It never hurts to be friendly with the neighbors!"

Meredith looked at him warily, then turned her attention to Wes. She couldn't read his face, but he didn't appear to be in distress. She relaxed somewhat.

"What have you two been talking about?"

"Shane has been telling me all about the restaurant industry," Wes interjected, a bit too brightly. "He knows quite a few important chefs. It's very impressive."

With caution, Meredith shifted her gaze to Shane, worried that he had sensed the irony in Wes's voice. Evidently he hadn't; he was still grinning.

"Did you know that The Gray Fox's duck confit is the vice president's favorite?" Wes continued, raising his eyebrows with mock appreciation. "I did not. I'll have to be sure to try it the next time I'm downtown."

"You should start thinking about making your reservation now," Shane told him. "At this time of year, the wait starts getting longer."

"Ah," said Wes. "I will keep that in mind."

Meredith was furious with both of them. What she had feared was a serious confrontation had ended up being nothing more than a pissing contest, Shane trying to one-up Wes by name-dropping and showing off, and Wes delighting in his own superior intelligence when it became clear that Shane was missing his sarcasm. She shook her head and asked herself why she bothered with men at all.

"Well, babe," Shane said, turning to Meredith and rubbing his hands together, "are you ready to go?"

Before she could answer, his phone rang. He pulled it out of his pocket and glanced at the screen, then held out his finger to tell them he'd be just a minute. He took a few steps into the middle of the street and turned his back to them while he took the call.

Wes was watching him grimly. When Shane was out of earshot, Wes turned to Meredith, his expression serious. "What the hell are you doing with this clown?" he asked her, without anger or harshness. He sounded genuinely concerned.

Meredith was taken aback. "What do you mean?"

"Come on, Meredith. You don't really have any feelings for this guy, do you?"

Meredith now understood why Wes was so much more at ease today. Having talked to Shane, he had discerned that he had nothing to worry about. He found Shane obtuse and full of hot air, as Meredith had, and as she had to admit she still did. He saw that between the two of them, he himself had the advantage. He was feeling more secure because he felt that he was better than Shane.

She turned to look back at Shane. He was still on the phone, his back still turned. She wondered who he was talking to.

Suddenly she felt Wes's hand on her shoulder. It sent a wave of warm shivers through her entire body. She let him turn her toward him, stunned. She realized her mouth was open, and she closed it. With caution she looked up into his face. She was struck by how handsome he was. Her heart fluttering madly, she instinctively prepared her lips for a kiss, having done so many times before in response to similar gestures.

But he had no intention of kissing her. He was studying her, his eyebrows forked downward. "It's me, Meredith. You can't fool me. I know why you're doing this." He retracted his hand and stood straight, his arms at his sides. "You're trying to take revenge on me for telling you not to see him again. Don't cut off your nose to spite your face. For once, just trust me. You don't want to have anything to do with him. He's not for you."

Meredith didn't like his telling her why she was doing anything or that she shouldn't be doing it. She felt she had had to tolerate enough of that when they were together; she certainly wasn't going to put up with it now. "Wes, as I said before, who I see in my own time is my decision. Please let me be."

"Damn it, Meredith, why can't you ever just trust me?" he exclaimed, his expression turning furious. "You always insist on doing things your way and in your own time. Well, look where that's gotten you! Come on, sweetheart," he said, his voice now pleading. "Don't do this. You know you're making a big mistake. Just stop being so hard-headed and do as I'm telling you. For everyone's sake."

Meredith didn't know what he was talking about anymore, but she didn't care. She was so put off by his overbearing smugness that she would have done anything he insisted she shouldn't. "Look where your insistence on doing things your way has gotten you," she said through clenched teeth. "You're just as alone as I am. Don't tell me what to do. Oh, and one more thing," she added before stalking off. "Don't call me 'sweetheart.'" With that, she joined Shane, who was just concluding his phone call. The two of them crossed the street and climbed into Shane's car, driving off, leaving Wes on the sidewalk to stare after them.

MEREDITH LOOKED out the passenger's side window, her elbow on the door and her fingers on her lips, deep in thought, for once glad that she and Shane didn't seem to have a lot to talk about. She regretted having spoken to Wes so harshly, but she believed he hadn't left her a choice. She had been viciously offended by the condescension in his voice, the suggestion that had she just done everything he had told her, they would be living in bliss, that all she had to do was sacrifice every opinion she had that was at odds with his.

Then she remembered how he had spoken in the present tense as if they were still together, how he had called her "sweetheart," and her fury turned to sympathy. She knew much of his anger was actually misdirected loneliness, that he had been speaking out of pain. She felt he was at the end of his rope, that he was making his last efforts to try to convince her that she had made a mistake in leaving him. He would never tell her so, but he could use Shane as a scapegoat. It looked like Shane was as convenient an escape for him as he was for her.

She didn't know why she made the decision to do it, but like so many decisions lately she went through with it before she had a chance to change her mind. She pulled her phone from her purse, not even feeling rude for doing so in front of Shane; he obviously didn't care, and neither did she.

She texted Wes: "I'm sorry."

Moments later she received his reply: "Me too."

~

SHANE AND MEREDITH had an uneventful date much like their previous two. Meredith at this point had stopped stressing about the conversation. The amount of conversation they were having was passable. It was enough to keep the evening lively but not enough to put any pressure on either of them to think too hard. Whereas before Meredith had worried about their lack of common interests, now she appreciated it. It meant she could retreat into her own thoughts.

As Shane parked in front of her house that night, he turned to her with a smile. "Well, I wish I could ask you out for tomorrow, but I can't. I'm spending the day at my sister's. I'm supposed to help her and her husband move some furniture, and then I'm going to cook them dinner. Hey," he exclaimed, opening his mouth and his eyes wide, and throwing his hands in the air. "You should come!"

Meredith couldn't suppress a grin. She had no reason to decline his invitation. "Okay," she said, and smiled. "Thanks."

"Awesome! But listen," he added, more seriously. "I'm going to take you up on your offer to meet me. It doesn't make sense for me to leave her house to come get you."

"That's fine. Where does she live?"

"Out near me in Maryland, toward Frederick."

"No problem. Why don't you text me the address and time?"

"Sounds good."

They sat awkwardly for a moment before Meredith spoke again.

"Thanks again for dinner. You've been very kind. I'd love to treat you sometime."

"It's nothing. I've got to eat, right? I might as well have company while I do it."

∼

MEREDITH KNEW from one of their conversations that Shane's sister Maribel was his twin. She was an interior decorator in a large firm in Frederick. She had been married to Peter, a CPA, for three years.

Meredith received Shane's text with Maribel's address that morning, directing her to be there at six o'clock. She dressed in a casual skirt and sweater, relishing the return of the warmer weather. Shane had told her it would take her forty-five minutes to get there, and she left her house a little early just in case she got lost.

An hour later she pulled into an affluent townhouse community, each lawn meticulously cared for and beautifully landscaped. Expensive cars sat in the driveways and in parking spots. She looked at the clock; it was six o'clock. She had hit no traffic and therefore had to conclude that the drive had taken her fifteen minutes longer than it took Shane because he drove too fast.

She was somewhat nervous to meet Maribel, but she felt more like she was meeting the sister of a friend than of a boyfriend.

Holding a torte she had made that morning, she strolled up to the Lachlans' townhouse and rang the bell.

The door was answered by a pretty, voluptuous woman of about her height. She had dark hair and rosy lips, and she wore cream-colored corduroy pants with a long, soft-looking white sweater. Her face was formed into pleasant smile of welcome.

"Hi, you must be Meredith," she said as she extended her arm to embrace her. Her voice was steady, sure, and confident. "I'm Maribel. It's nice to meet you! Shane has told us a lot about you."

Meredith wondered what Shane possibly could have told Maribel; she had shared barely anything about herself in the three weeks she had known him. She returned Maribel's smile and embrace as she was drawn inside.

"It's nice to meet you too. Thank you so much for having me."

"Oh, I love meeting Shane's friends! They're always so interesting. What's this?" she asked as Meredith handed her the torte. "That looks beautiful! Do you do a lot of cooking?"

"Yes," Meredith answered as Maribel led her through the house. She laughed. "Though not as much as your brother, of course."

"I'm sure Shane told you that our mother graduated from The Culinary Institute," Maribel said as she placed the torte on the kitchen counter. "She was going to be a great chef herself until she married Dad and was swept up in the political life. That's why she was so excited when Shane went into cooking. We're all good cooks, though of course Shane is the best."

Meredith hadn't known any of this. She was about to say so when Shane strode in, followed by a tall, gloomy-looking gentleman who Meredith assumed was Peter. He was somewhat lanky, his khaki pants and white sweater making him look even more drawn. His features might have been handsome had he not been so gaunt; his chin was prominent, as was his nose, but his eyes were large, bright, and blue. He struck her as someone who kept his distance from company and crowds—maybe it was the way he walked behind Shane, even in his own house.

"Hey, babe," Shane announced as he approached. He stopped a couple of feet in front of her, his eyes wide and his hands on his hips. Once again he was wearing jeans and a t-shirt, this one black with a modern-looking print splattered across the shoulder. "I'm sure Maribel has been taking good care of you. Peter and I just moved that bookcase from the basement. It was heavier than I had thought," he said, and clenched his hands together, as if in pain. "If I had known it was going to be so heavy, I would have stayed home."

"You'd never do that," said Maribel. "You know we've got too much on you."

Out of the corner of her eye, Meredith noticed a piano in the formal living room next door. She turned to Shane and smiled.

"Would you play something for us?"

Shane looked taken aback. "What? Me?"

"Of course." Meredith remembered how adeptly he had played at The Gray Fox, how easily his fingers had trickled over the keys and how fluid was the music that had filled the room. "You played so beautifully at your restaurant the night we first met."

"Shane doesn't play," explained Maribel. "At least, not unless he's forced to. It's a shame, though, as he's really very good."

Peter was lumbering over to a small table that held a bottle of wine and four glasses. When he had reached his destination, he poured the wine and returned to the others, wordlessly handing a glass to each of them.

"I almost forgot Peter," said Maribel. "Meredith, this is my husband."

Peter raised his glass in salute but said nothing.

"Well, let's start dinner," Shane said, rubbing his hands together. "I'm starving."

"I'm excited to see you cook," Meredith told him, smiling brightly. "It will be fun to see the chef in action."

"Don't tell him that," Maribel said, placing her hand on Meredith's arm. "You'll give him a big head."

"Be nice," said Shane.

Shane made swordfish steaks on a stovetop grill and accompanied them with pineapple salsa, gingered rice, and a simple green salad. They sat down in the dining room to eat, the table having already been set with elegant gray dishes on bamboo placemats, the soft light of the falling evening pouring in through the glass doors in the back of the house.

"Maribel, I hear you're an interior decorator," Meredith said. "It isn't hard to believe. Your house is beautiful."

"Thanks, Meredith. We just bought this place a couple of years ago. It was fun to be able to decorate my own home instead of somebody else's. And what is it that you do?"

Meredith was a little surprised that Shane had not at least told Maribel that she was a teacher; it was one of the only things he knew about her. Once again she wondered what it was he had told her. "I teach high school English," she replied.

"English was my favorite subject in school. I'm glad to hear that about you."

Meredith smiled, grateful to Maribel for making her feel comfortable.

Her eyes widened as she tasted Shane's dinner. "Shane—this is amazing!"

"Thank you."

"It's much better than the fish I had at the restaurant," she added, and grinned.

"I didn't actually cook that fish. That's why."

"What are you talking about?" asked Maribel.

"Meredith ate at The Gray Fox a few weeks ago. That's how we met. She basically told me my food was terrible."

"Oh!" Meredith exclaimed in protest, flushing, but going along with the joke. "I was just trying to be helpful."

"She told me what I was doing wrong and what she'd do to fix it. Then she told me she made my meatloaf and that it was terrible, too."

"Remind me why you two are dating?" Maribel asked, looking between them with raised eyebrows.

Shane and Meredith stared at each other for a moment or two.

Shane smiled then. He said, "Meredith was wearing a pretty dress. I'm weak."

"Well," said Maribel, dabbing her lips with her napkin, "unless she plans on wearing that dress every day, you'd better find another reason."

Peter had been silent this entire time. He had barely looked up from his plate. Meredith wanted to engage him in conversation but decided against it. She had a feeling it was understood that he should be left alone.

They continued dinner, chatting casually until Shane rose to clear the plates and clean up, leaving Maribel, Meredith, and Peter at the table.

"So, Meredith," Maribel began, her elbows pointed on the table, her hands folding under her chin. "Shane tells me your father is Harold Beck. That's quite a coincidence."

"Yes, it is. It could make for some awkwardness, but I'm sure it won't be a problem."

Maribel's eyes sharpened slyly, and her mouth pulled up a little at the corner. She studied Meredith for several moments before addressing her again. "Meredith, can I speak candidly with you?"

"Sure," Meredith responded, growing anxious.

Maribel pursed her lips and stared at the table, gathering her thoughts. "How can I put this," she said to herself, strumming her fingers against each other. Finally she looked at Meredith and shook her head. "Never mind. I'll tell you what," she said then, smiling once more. "Let's just see what happens, and if you encounter a problem just talk to me about it. Okay?"

"Okay," Meredith agreed nervously.

Meredith felt herself being watched. She looked up only to find Peter staring at her. When their eyes met, he cast his back downward.

Shane reentered the room carrying four small plates and Meredith's torte. He carved four slices and served each of them, then poured four cups of coffee and placed one next to each plate. Meredith didn't want to watch him taste the torte but couldn't help glancing at him out of the corner of her eye. She saw his eyebrows rise as he chewed slowly at first and then more naturally; he swallowed and dove in for another bite. He didn't comment, but Meredith was satisfied with his reaction.

"This is great, Meredith," Maribel said, with a polite smile. "Is it your recipe?"

"I have to admit it's not. It's Angeline Halpren's, but I've modified it somewhat."

"No wonder," Shane mumbled, wiping his fingers on his napkin. He swallowed, then said, "I thought it was heavy on the spice. Her recipes always are."

"That's probably my fault," Meredith said, a little unnerved but pushing that feeling aside. "I added cloves, but the recipe didn't call for it."

"Huh," Shane said, returning his attention to the torte.

After they finished dessert, they sat around the table talking. Maribel told Meredith that their family always had a big Easter dinner at their parents' house in Frederick and that she was sure they would be delighted to have her. Meredith braved a glance at Shane, worried that he would be upset that Maribel had taken it upon herself to invite her; however, he seemed perfectly content. He was leaning back in his chair, his feet pushing it onto its back two legs, his face lifted toward the ceiling and his arms folded on his chest.

"It's a big ordeal," Maribel told her. "They have lots of family and friends there. I have a couple of other friends going, too. It should be fun."

"Oh yeah, it'll be a blast," said Shane, his chair landing on all fours with a heavy thud. "Dad regaling everyone with stories about his acquisitions and accomplishments, and bitching about the president, and Mom ordering everyone around with that pissed off look of hers. I can't wait."

Meredith stared at him.

"Shane!" Maribel scolded. "Now that's not nice. And you're going to scare off poor Meredith." She looked to Meredith and cocked her head in apology. "Don't mind Shane. He's always making everything seem worse than it really is."

Shane shrugged but said no more; he was picking up torte crumbs with his finger and licking them off.

It grew late, and Meredith thanked them for a lovely evening and stood to head home. Shane walked her outside, where she bristled against the cold; it had grown quite chilly since the sun had set.

He followed her to her car and stood beside her at the driver's side door, his hands in his pockets as he stared down at her.

Meredith said, "Thanks for inviting me to meet your sister, Shane. I had a really nice time. She's wonderful." She smiled warmly but wrapped her arms around herself, shivering.

"No problem."

They passed an awkward moment in silence.

"Well," Meredith said, looking at her car and then back at Shane, "I'd better go."

"Okay," he said. "Hey," he added suddenly.

"Yes?"

"Is it still too soon to kiss you?"

Meredith felt her heart drop to the ground. Even if it had been too soon, which she finally had begun to feel it wasn't, his simple question and sincere expression would have changed her mind. She had yet to figure him out, had felt tonight more than ever that they had a long way to go before they understood each other—but she had been more at ease with him tonight regardless, had enjoyed the glimpse into his background and had appreciated his having invited her to see it.

She looked at him, really studying his features, his thick neck and wide cheekbones, sensuously full lips—she had never noticed quite how full they were—and large eyes, his lashes so long as to make his eyes look almost feminine. They were the one soft feature about him. Everything else was almost too masculine, too angular and too powerful.

She did want to kiss him but was afraid to want to. She had promised herself she was not going to fall in love again. She wasn't truly worried about falling in love with Shane—she sensed that, while they could get along well if they worked at it, they were operating from two very different perspectives. But she didn't want to confuse herself. Though she didn't think she'd ever fall in love with Shane, she did worry that she would begin to grow dependent on him, and what then? She didn't know him well enough to know how loyal he would be, whether he would stay with her through the ups and downs of normal relationships, or whether he would leave her at the first sign of a challenge or at the first flirtatious look from another woman. Standing there, watching him waiting for her response, she knew she was thinking too hard. In her mind she imagined him telling her, *It's just a kiss, Meredith*.

She had already decided he could kiss her but hadn't had the courage to say so. Shane seemed to know this and leaned in toward her. Meredith felt the heat off his body before she felt his lips on hers and was unprepared for but delighted by how his nearness shielded her from the cold of the evening. To her surprise, his lips brushed hers lightly, and nothing more; he did not linger, but pulled away and stared at her, his eyes still serious but also touched by something like tenderness. He smiled then and rubbed her cold arms with his large, rough hands. Instantly she felt warmer, and she returned his gaze starry-eyed.

"I'll call you," he said, and removed his hands.

"Okay," she responded softly, dazed.

He took a couple of steps backward, then waved and returned his hands to his pockets. He walked back up toward the house, entered, and closed the door, not waiting for her to drive off, not even waiting for her to step into her car.

MEREDITH TRIED NOT to think too hard on the way home. She turned on some music and zoned out, letting her mind wander. When she arrived home, she noticed that Wes's living room light was on. She wearily climbed out of the car and went right upstairs to her bedroom, where she changed and washed for bed, ready to fall asleep as soon as her head hit the pillow.

On an impulse, though, she went to her bedroom window and looked across the street. Wes's living room was now dark, as was his bedroom. Meredith knew he had been waiting until she returned home. She felt as if she should have resented his keeping tabs on her, but she could only appreciate his looking out for her. Somehow Wes's being right across the street made her feel safe. Thinking of this as she climbed into bed, she grew afraid and put it out of her mind. It was better to feel alone in her passionless relationship than to be tempted by love. She didn't want to begin comparing what could be with what actually was. She didn't want to think the thoughts that might make her doubt the wisdom of her decision.

CHAPTER FIVE

THE THAYERS

*A*pril came around, and with it the prospect of Meredith's spring break. She and Shane continued seeing each other once or twice on weekends. By now they had been dating for almost six weeks. Nothing had changed. They went out for formal lunches and dinners, involving themselves in superficial conversations and joking with each other, Shane entertaining and confusing her with his odd, spontaneous sense of humor, and Meredith still not quite understanding what it was about her that had drawn him to her. He was cordial and polite with her, but he still didn't seem to care very much about her life. He never asked her how her day had been or how her job was going. He knew nothing about Nancy or the school play. Meredith had tried to summarize the situation for him, but she had given up halfway through her explanation when it had become clear that he wasn't really paying attention.

Still, he appeared to enjoy her company, and he seemed to want to impress her. She let him do it, happy for the distraction. He had kissed her several more times, each time with a little more enthusiasm, but overall their relationship remained without much physical contact. Meredith was satisfied; she was having a good time. She was attracted to Shane but not desperately so; she liked the tease, but she didn't feel the wait was unbearable. It was the perfect balance. She felt a little sad when she considered that Shane apparently felt the same about her, attracted enough to want to kiss her but not enough to feel inclined to hold her hand or rub her knee—but she was content to take it slowly and was grateful that he wasn't pressuring her.

Meredith had spoken to Tara at length about him. Tara didn't understand what Meredith was doing. She wanted Meredith to break it off with him and have some time to herself. She was worried that Meredith would wither away with Shane. She was suspicious of Shane's patience with her, wondering why it was that an attractive man who was relatively well-known would choose to spend his time with a woman who would barely even kiss him, when he probably could have any woman he wanted.

Meredith chose not to worry about these things. It was working for her, and that was all that mattered. In spite of the odd silences between them, they had grown more comfortable around each other and had fallen into their own strange routine. It had become safe, familiar, and free from stress, which was exactly what Meredith had wanted.

One thing that did bother Meredith was the growing competition between Shane and Wes. Now that the weather was warmer, her neighbors were almost always out in the evenings, and it was rare that they didn't see Wes at some point as they were heading out or returning home from a date. The two men always shot each other knowing glances and strutted a little more proudly in each other's presence. They had had one more conversation, and Meredith didn't know whether to be annoyed or amused. They reminded her of two roosters competing for the attention of a single hen.

Meredith missed Wes's companionship. Often she found herself smiling when she recalled his hearty laugh and his cheerful confidence, then turning sad once more as she imagined him going about his days alone.

In addition, as spring break approached, Meredith grew nervous; her heart fluttered when she remembered her previous spring break. She couldn't help but lie in bed and imagine that Nick was lying there with her, recalling with vivid, breathtaking detail their final night together, how he had gone through such pain to resist her, finally resolving to make the most of the time they had left. In the note he had written her, he had said it had been the best night of his life, and Meredith had to agree. It had seemed as if they had collected all the passion, understanding, and comfort of their entire relationship and compressed it together into a few short hours. Never before or since had she felt so close to anyone.

She was now at a point where she felt that she was betraying Nick when her thoughts turned to Wes and that she was betraying Wes when her thoughts turned to Nick. She wondered if she'd ever work through her feelings for either of them. She felt lost and ill at ease, once again mourning a loss as the green buds of spring announced the birth of a new season. Frustrated, she was driven even further to Shane, for whom she had much simpler feelings and with whom such thoughtfulness was not required, or even advisable.

MEREDITH DECLINED to spend Easter with the Thayers, having decided to join Tara and her family instead. However, she did accept Shane's invitation to his parents' house for dinner the following Saturday night.

She enjoyed her Easter this year, happy not to feel the need to excuse herself to cry every five minutes. Grace and Frank were not in attendance; Tara informed Meredith that they were somewhere in the Southwest and were planning on returning home sometime before the fall. Meredith felt a jolt of panic. She had not once considered that when Grace and Frank returned, she would need to find a new place to live. She wondered if Grace and Frank were still interested in selling the home to her. Then she wondered if she'd even be interested in buying it. She decided not to worry about it until she had more details. It was impossible to gauge where her life would be in several months' time.

She spent her spring break relaxing and enjoying the warm weather. One afternoon she was reading on her front porch when Wes's car glided down the street, slowing as it pulled into his driveway. The door swung open, and he emerged, wearing gray suit slacks and a dress shirt and tie. He waved at her as he shut the door; then he opened the back door and withdrew his jacket and briefcase. Meredith watched him. Suddenly she was on her feet, her book laid on the table beside her; before she knew it she was in the middle of the street, and then on his lawn, not knowing how she had gotten there, right in front of him as he made his way around to the other side of his car. He was standing still, watching her. As she approached, his face grew more serious. His eyes followed her every move.

"Hi, Wes," she said precariously, not knowing how he would receive her.

"Hi, sweetheart," he responded, and Meredith's heart warmed.

"Can we be friends?" she asked, tired of tiptoeing around.

"I'd like that, Meredith," he said. "I've been meaning to talk to you for a long time." He placed his briefcase on the ground and laid his jacket on top. He stuck his hands in his pockets and leaned against his car. "I just haven't had the courage to go over there."

"I understand. I'm over here on a whim. I didn't know if you'd want to see me."

His expression remained serious. "Of course I want to see you," he said, his voice heavy with feeling. His eyes narrowed as he studied her, and his lips turned up into a mild grin. "I don't suppose you've reconsidered, have you?"

Meredith's eyes misted, and she frowned. She didn't know what to say, and therefore said nothing.

Wes's half-hearted grin dissipated. "I didn't think so. But I had to ask."

Meredith was controlling her tears with effort. Hurting Wes felt like a knife through her heart.

"Meredith, you know—" He paused, frowning.

He seemed to have something important to say, and Meredith waited. But he never said it. He sighed, finally, and smiled, but the smile looked forced.

"It's nothing. Well, I'd better go inside. Thanks for coming over to see me. I'm glad we had this little talk."

"Me too," she said cheerfully, trying to help him lighten the mood. "I guess I'll see you around."

"I guess so. Goodnight, Meredith."

"Goodnight."

She turned and walked back across the street. When she arrived at her front door, she turned toward Wes's house before going inside. He was nowhere to be seen.

THAT WEEKEND MEREDITH drove over an hour to the Thayers' home in Frederick. She was nervous. She thought about nothing but her anxiety the entire way there, unable to enjoy the journey at all. Meeting a partner's family never was easy. She would have thought this time that she would be less worried, given the relaxed nature of her relationship with Shane. But she had an uneasy feeling about the Thayers. She had gathered that tension existed between them and Shane, and she wasn't sure what to expect.

She wasn't even sure who was going to be there. She knew

for certain she would meet Shane's mother Tess and his older brother Roger. Maribel and Peter would be there, and of course Shane. Senator John Thayer had another engagement and may put in an appearance toward the end. Shane had told her that one or two additional friends might join them, but he had been vague, and Meredith didn't know whether he wasn't sure of the details himself or simply wasn't bothering to inform her of them.

When she arrived that afternoon, she sat parked on the side of the road for a moment, staring at the house. It was situated in an affluent neighborhood outside Frederick, Maryland, what appeared to be a carefully planned development of luxury homes with ample space dividing the sizable properties. The trees looked young; they were thin and sparse, offering a wide view of the surrounding land. The Thayers' house was brick with white trim and tall curved windows on each of the two floors. In the center were black double doors, crowned with a wide curved window and surrounded by narrow white columns, two on each side. The landscaping was symmetrical on either side of the house, dominated by trimmed bushes and oversized urns. The main part of the house was flanked by two recessed extensions, each window adorned with a narrow dormer.

For some reason it was exactly what Meredith had expected. Its magnitude intimidated her, and she wondered what she was doing there. She sucked in her breath and collected her lemon cake from the passenger's seat, then climbed out of the car. Straightening her linen skirt and blue blouse, she walked up the brick walkway to the front door. She rang the doorbell and waited, her heart thumping.

Maribel answered the door, and Meredith breathed a sigh of relief. She heard animated voices in the background but tried to focus on Shane's sister, who looked stunning in a form-fitting brown dress.

"Hi, Meredith," she said with a bright smile, and hugged her.

"Glad you could make it. Shane's in the kitchen with the others. Come on in and meet everyone."

Meredith handed Maribel her cake and followed her into the house. The open floor plan meant that every sound was heard throughout the entire floor, and she felt that the clicking of her heels was unbearably loud. The house was decorated with over-sized, heavy furniture and serious artwork in reds and golds; even the drapes were dark and heavy. It was tasteful but grand, and it seemed as if it were trying to be so.

Meredith stepped into the massive kitchen to find about a dozen people standing around in mild conversation, each holding a glass of wine and staring at her as she entered the room. Shane, wearing dark slacks and a gray shirt that was pulled tautly over his broad frame, was at the stove slinging pans, removing pots from the oven, and putting the finishing touches on large trays of food. A woman in nondescript clothes was with him, wordlessly following his short, quiet directions. When he reached for a spoon several feet from where he was standing, he glimpsed her out of the corner of his eye.

"Hey, babe. Glad you made it," he said as she stepped toward him. He switched out two pans of food, then brusquely turned. "Hey, this is Meredith," he announced to the room at large as he wiped his hands on a dishtowel. His forehead was sweating, and he wiped that too.

They all nodded politely and murmured greetings.

Shane pointed around the circle with an extended finger, quickly introducing each guest. Meredith recognized Peter, who was standing behind, and also another man, who she correctly assumed was Shane's older brother Roger; the two looked nearly identical, the only difference being that Roger was fairer, his hair lighter and his build less severe than Shane's.

From a doorway off to the side entered a woman Meredith was certain was Shane's mother Tess. Dark-haired like Shane and Maribel, she was of average height with a stern face and slender build, which she had dressed in a black suit that belted around the waist.

Meredith turned toward Tess with nervous expectation, the beginnings of a smile on her face as she prepared to be introduced. But Tess didn't seem to notice her standing there, and she approached Shane with soft steps.

She sighed as she planted her feet together next to Shane and proceeded to help him stir, pour, and prepare.

Meredith waited for Shane to introduce her or for Tess to look in her direction so she might smile by way of greeting, but she was left waiting, and she felt uncomfortable, as if she should introduce herself but not wanting to interrupt their work. She looked around for Maribel and spotted her speaking to a couple of women several feel away.

When Maribel noticed that Meredith was by herself and that Tess was standing nearby, she excused herself from her friends and approached.

"Mom, did you meet Meredith?" she asked, placing her hand on her mother's shoulder and turning her.

Tess's eyes finally met Meredith's. Her expression remained unchanged.

"Thank you for having me, Mrs. Thayer," Meredith said brightly, determined to be friendly in spite of this cold reception. "It's so nice to finally meet you."

"A pleasure," Tess replied as she turned back to Shane. "Make yourself at home," she added over her shoulder. She slipped an oven mitt over her hand and bent to withdraw something from the oven.

Meredith bristled but was encouraged by Maribel, who now placed her hand on Meredith's waist and drew her out of the way. "Here, Meredith," she said. "Let me introduce you to my friends."

Meredith and Maribel made their way to the center of the room, where Maribel tapped the shoulders of the women to whom she had been speaking earlier. Meredith recalled that Shane had introduced them as Bridget and Caroline.

"Hi, girls. I thought we could get to know each other a little better while we waited for dinner."

Bridget and Caroline smiled politely, but their expressions were cool. Caroline was staring at Meredith with wide, sharp eyes. Her face was frozen, almost plastic, and Meredith had the absurd feeling that Caroline already disliked her.

She nodded and greeted them with a smile but was growing more and more desperate for the night to be over. She yearned for the warmth of the Bickharts, remembering how Sarah had pulled her aside and spoken to her with such sincerity about her appreciation for what she had done for Wes, how their delighted voices had carried across the table as they reminisced about happy times, how she had imagined being a part of their family one day. Her eyes searched for Shane, the comfort he could provide a distant second to Wes's but familiar nonetheless, and therefore safer than the hostility of the women around her.

Shane and his mother were working together to gather the dishes for dinner, their movements almost synchronized, and Meredith had to appreciate the deftness and skill with which they worked. The nondescript woman, whom by now Meredith took to be a housekeeper, had vanished into the dining room. Meredith stood silently, registering the voices of Maribel and her friends but not paying attention; she was too busy composing herself.

Finally Shane and Tess began removing dishes from the kitchen and transferring them to the dining room next door. Meredith straightened her back and took a step toward them, prepared to offer to help, but Maribel held her back.

"Just stay here," she whispered.

After a few minutes Shane announced that they were ready, and the guests headed toward the dining room. Shane waited in the doorway for Meredith, who was last. She looked up toward him, seeking reassurance in his face. He smiled dimly, and his hand guided her out of the room.

Tess sat at the head of the table, Roger at the other end. The remainder of the guests filtered in on either side, Shane sitting to his mother's right and Meredith beside him. Maribel sat on her other side, Peter beside Maribel. Just across the table from Meredith was Caroline, whose face wore a dark smile that gave Meredith shivers.

The nondescript woman by now had changed into a plain black dress, and she hurried around the room placing soup bowls at each place.

"Tess, thank you for having us," Caroline said as they all settled in, her smile widening and now displaying something close to warmth. "It's so kind of you to host two weekends in a row. I know it must be tedious for you, but at least it means I get to see you twice."

"Oh, it's no trouble, Caroline, dear," Tess told her, her face softening, an effect Meredith hadn't thought possible for her. "I'm happy to see you too. It's a little tiring at this time of year, I have to admit—but as last weekend wasn't convenient for everyone, I was obliged to entertain again."

Meredith blushed. She wasn't certain Tess was referring to her declining to attend the Thayers' Easter dinner, but she was growing more and more uneasy and had begun getting the feeling she was meeting Shane's family already at a disadvantage.

"Well, it's very kind of you, Tess."

"Thank you, Caroline. You're sweet."

Meredith looked at Caroline, whose eyes darted toward her and then back toward Tess.

They began eating the soup in silence.

Tess said, "Caroline, how is school?"

"It's going well, thank you. We're preparing for standardized exams. Last year my students' scores were highest in the school."

"That's wonderful, though it doesn't surprise me," said Tess. "Good luck this year. I know you'll be successful again."

"Caroline is a fourth-grade teacher," Shane said to Meredith, turning to her. Then he turned to his mother. "Mom, Meredith is a teacher too. She teaches high school English." He faced Meredith once again and smiled. "Isn't that right?"

"Yes," Meredith said gratefully. "I have one of each grade, nine through twelve."

"I enjoy teaching the younger children," said Caroline, her voice tinged with challenge. "I'm reaching them during their formative years. By the time they get to high school, they're already so cynical."

"I wouldn't say that," Meredith said with a smile, keeping her voice bright. "They're just a bit more wise to the world. But I haven't found them to be cynical at all. If anything, they're eager to learn how to make sense of everything they know."

"It's not a competition," Tess pronounced, glancing at Meredith and then back down to her soup. She scooped some soup onto her spoon and continued questioning Caroline. "What will you do this summer? Are you traveling again?"

"No, actually. This summer I'm volunteering at a day camp for children in need. I just want to give back this year. I think that's so important." Her eyes darted toward Meredith once more.

"That is very noble of you, Caroline. It's too bad there aren't more people like you. The world would be a much better place." Tess turned to Meredith and addressed her directly for the first time, her eyes focusing sharply on her. "What about you, Meredith? What are your plans for the summer?"

Meredith had the feeling she was being tested and wished she had a better answer to give her. "To be honest, I'm not sure yet," she replied, trying to sound confident. "Last summer I was in the process of moving, and my time was occupied with my personal affairs. This is my first summer in Washington. I've really enjoyed working one-on-one with students this year. I suppose I'll look into tutoring, now that summer is approaching."

Tess's eyebrows rose. "Yes, it certainly is. Maybe Caroline can help give you a boost."

Meredith and Caroline exchanged glances. Caroline attempted a smile, but it appeared more like a grimace. "Yes," she said. "Of course."

Meredith was wondering what was going on here; she was becoming more and more convinced with each passing moment that there was something she was missing, that she already had been the target of displeasure before she ever walked through the door. She tried to be conciliatory. "Caroline, I'd love to talk to you later about whether your school has implemented any changes since the new education bill was passed. I'm always curious to hear how other schools are faring."

"Oh, we know all about your views on this, Meredith," Tess announced, her chin lifted, the words pouring from her with force as if she had been holding them inside for some time. "That is, if your views coincide with those of your father, which I am assuming they do." She glared at her, her eyes dark. "Do they?"

Meredith suddenly understood, and she felt fire burn within her. "Yes, they do," she said, "but I'm always open to hearing other points of view. It's impossible to formulate an educated opinion without gathering all the facts."

"How true a statement that is," Tess agreed, but her voice was dripping with irony. "If only everyone felt that way."

Not missing the insult to her father, Meredith couldn't prevent a frown from creeping onto her face. Though she and her father had rarely gotten along, and though she had felt the sting of his inattention for as long as she could remember, she respected him for his beliefs and for having the courage to stand up for them, and she would fight against anybody on his behalf.

"Most people I've come across do," she said, with a forced

smile, trying to diffuse the tension and avoid confrontation. "It's just important to keep an open mind."

"Unfortunately even people with open minds can be misguided," interjected Roger from the other end of the table. "It's all about interpretation of fact. The same fact can be spun any which way, according to agenda. The problem is when agendas become law."

At that moment the housekeeper returned and began clearing soup bowls. The conversation switched to another topic.

"Shane," said Tess, turning to her son, "did the magazine ever call you back about your interview?"

"No."

"Have you followed up with them?"

"They told me they'd get back to me in a week if they were going to use me. Considering it's been over a month, I think it's safe to say they don't have any interest."

"Maybe there's something I can do."

The table was silent after that, but Meredith felt the anxiety rise. She sensed heat radiating off of Shane, and she felt a wave of sympathy for him. She knew what it was like to grow up in a house in which accomplishments were never enough, in which there was always more to be done and something else with which to be disappointed. In a flash she remembered the look on her father's face when Vince had told him he was going to be a painter. She gently placed her hand on Shane's thigh in a gesture of comfort. He turned his head in her direction and then faced his mother once more.

"You don't have to do anything. If I wanted to call them back, I'd call them myself."

"But you won't. Let me at least try. I may be able to have some influence."

"Get off my back, Mom. I'm thirty years old. I think I can handle this myself."

Tess put her hands up in the air in surrender, her eyebrows lifted high and her lips drawn downward.

"Shane, I made your cream puff pie last night," Caroline said then, her voice suddenly sweet and high. "It was so good! I was going to bring it with me today, but I ate the whole thing!"

Meredith had to grin as the entire picture became clear to her now. She looked intently at Caroline, for the first time noticing how she was gazing at Shane with wide blue eyes and a coy smile, the way her body was turned toward him just so, the way she had arranged her smooth blond hair prettily over one shoulder. She realized that Caroline was in love with Shane and that Tess was doing everything in her power to throw the two of them together, that she herself was nothing more than an annoying interference with a nuisance of a father to boot. Somehow knowing this gave her confidence; she felt now that she knew the enemy she was fighting and could formulate a plan, or at least set up her defenses. The unidentifiable tension had been brutal; a love triangle was irritating but easily tolerated with the right approach.

"I haven't tried that recipe," Meredith said, attempting to play the game. "It sounds delicious, though. I like to think desserts are my strength."

"Caroline, you'll have to swim a hundred extra laps to make up for it," Tess said, ignoring Meredith. "You don't want to lose that lovely figure of yours."

Meredith smirked. So this was the way it was going to be. She was happy to have figured out the Thayers. She could handle a fight of which she knew the rules. The only question was whether she wanted to fight it.

AFTER DINNER they all moved to the living room. Shane and Meredith fell into a conversation with Maribel, who told them she recently had had the honor of decorating a house for clients who owned an original Degas. Meredith was delighted. She and Maribel began their own conversation as Shane drifted off to speak with Roger. A grand piano sat heavily in a corner of the room, lid open, as if waiting to be played—but no one did, and Meredith decided against mentioning it.

After some time Maribel asked Meredith if she would like to see her parents' Cassatt. Meredith's eyes opened wide with surprise and eagerness, and she let Maribel lead her upstairs to her parents' bedroom. She felt ill at ease in this room, but she focused her attention on the work of art in front of her and forgot her anxiety.

"This is beautiful," she said breathlessly. "How did your parents come to own it?"

"It was my grandmother's," Maribel told her, her arms folded as she stared at the painting. "She acquired it when she was in Europe."

"It's stunning," Meredith said, and was silent for some time as she studied it. She turned to Maribel and smiled. "Thank you for showing it to me."

"You're welcome," Maribel said, returning her smile.

They said nothing for several moments, but the air was tense with unspoken thoughts.

Maribel spoke first. "So have we scared you off yet?" she asked, grinning mischievously.

Meredith shrugged. "No," she said, turning to Maribel. "I can handle a little tension." Her expression turned thoughtful. "I take it your mother prefers Caroline for Shane. How long has this been going on?"

"Forever," Maribel said, relaxing her stance. "My father and Caroline's father went to college together, and I've known her for a long time. Mom's always wanted to see them together, but Shane hasn't wanted to settle down. Plus there's the problem of Caroline's father."

"What's the problem with Caroline's father?"

"He can't stand Shane. He thinks he's going nowhere and that he has no ambition."

Meredith raised her eyebrows. "I think Shane's done pretty well for himself, with the restaurant and the show and all."

Maribel looked at Meredith carefully. She said, "Yes, that's true," but she seemed distracted.

Meredith waited for her to say more, but they stood in silence. Finally Meredith said, "I wasn't expecting such hostility over my father. I hope they can get past it."

"Don't worry about that. My father will be home soon. He's usually a bit more reasonable about these things. Hang in there, Meredith. You'll be fine."

They walked side by side out of the room and down the stairs and joined the others in the living room. They were sitting now, and as the two women entered the room Shane shifted on the couch and held out his arm for her to sit next to him. She joined him willingly and snuggled in, surprised when she felt a shiver of excitement as she pressed herself against him. She wasn't used to being this close to him, and as their hips touched and her back met his chest and waist, she delighted in the way her blood tingled at the physical contact, which she had missed since her split with Wes two months before.

Meredith searched the room for Caroline and found her sitting straight and tall in an armchair to the side, her eyes dark with contempt. Meredith's own face instantly turned serious, and it was only when she frowned that she realized how widely she had been smiling.

Maribel said, "Meredith, have you cooked anything interesting lately?"

"Nothing interesting enough to report on," Meredith responded. Suddenly she was hit with a thought. "Oh!" she cried. "I brought a lemon cake, but it wasn't put out."

"Suzanne must have forgotten it," Tess said blandly. "Sorry."

"It's all right; I just wanted to make sure you knew it was

here." She smiled. "You can have it for breakfast. I don't know about you, but I like to indulge in a little cake for breakfast every now and then. It would be great with a cup of coffee."

Tess's lips made the faintest effort to turn up at the corners, reflecting a pathetically unpleasant smile; the rest of her face wore a grim, annoyed look.

Meredith gave up. She had no desire to try to appease people who were not to be appeased. It just wasn't worth it. She wanted to continue seeing Shane, but she had more interest in her integrity than in him, and she wasn't about to let herself be degraded and insulted. Had she had stronger feelings for Shane she might have considered it, but as it was, the stakes just weren't high enough. He was a fun friend, but she could have dinner with anyone.

Just as she was getting ready to excuse herself and go home, all heads snapped up at the sound of the front door opening and slamming shut. They waited as heavy footsteps tread through the house, finally sounding closer and closer until Senator Thayer, silver-haired, tall, and strong like his sons, was standing in the doorway.

"Greetings, friends and family," Senator Thayer bellowed cheerfully, looking around the room to assess who was there. His eyes fell on Meredith. "And who might you be?"

"Dad, this is Meredith," Shane said. "Meredith Beck."

The senator's eyes opened wide, and he grinned. "Aha," he said, and pointed at her. "Shane told me he had met you. And how is old Harold these days? Still griping about complicated issues he knows nothing about?"

"Dad," Shane said, his voice dark. "Lay off."

"No, no," the senator said with contrived laughter. "I'm only teasing. I'm sure you're a very nice girl. I don't have any beef with you in spite of your unfortunate lineage. What did Mr. Beck have to say in that editorial, anyway? Let me think," said Senator Thayer, in a grand performance, holding his chin in his fingers much as Shane had on their date at The Spring House, though Meredith was certain he had memorized every word of the editorial. "I believe he said my bill was 'foolishly short-sighted, dangerously ignorant, and stubbornly partisan.'" He looked at Meredith. "Does that sound about right?"

Meredith looked back at the senator in silence, exhausted.

Shane stood then and faced his father. "What the hell is your problem? You've been home for five minutes, and already you're giving one of your speeches."

"Shane!" Tess exclaimed. "What has gotten into you?"

Shane turned to her. "Don't act like you don't know what I'm talking about. You're no better than he is. What is the matter with everyone? Christ! Just lighten up!"

Everyone stared at him in shock, Meredith included. She had no time to think about what was happening, however, for he grabbed her hand and pulled her up from the couch and out of the room, barely giving her enough time to pick up her purse as he led her out the front door.

Once outside, he slowed until they were standing on the sidewalk in front of the house, which loomed impassively behind them. They faced each other. Shane was breathing heavily and stood looking at the house for a moment while he calmed himself.

Finally his eyes met hers.

"My family's the worst," he spat. "I'm sorry. I should have warned you."

She sighed and attempted to smile. "It's not your fault. But thank you for standing up for me. And for pulling me out of there," she added with a sly smile. "Please say goodnight to Maribel for me. I don't want her to think I didn't appreciate her kindness."

Shane didn't appear to be paying much attention; he was staring back at the house. Meredith cautiously touched his arm, and he emerged from his dark reverie and looked at her.

"All right," he said. "I guess you'd better go. I'll call you, if that's okay."

"That's okay," she said, smiling in earnest this time. "Thanks for inviting me tonight. You tried."

Without another word, he took her shoulders in his hands and kissed her, this time with more force and enthusiasm than he ever had before. She closed her eyes, letting herself become lost in the moment until she felt his hand on her breast.

She pulled sharply away.

"Sorry," he said. "I wasn't sure. It's cool."

He kissed her forehead and took a few steps back, then smiled and waved. He stalked back up to the house, then stepped inside and closed the door, leaving Meredith standing alone on the sidewalk in front of her car.

~

"DUMP HIS ASS," said Tara.

Meredith was making the long drive home and figured there was no better way to work through her feelings than by talking them over with her best friend.

"Tell me how you really feel," Meredith joked.

"I'm serious, Merry. What are you thinking? You are tolerating way too much here. You can do so much better!"

Meredith knew Tara was right, but she was afraid to tell her friend her real reasons for staying with Shane.

At her silence, Tara calmed herself and grew more thoughtful. "What's going on with you, Merry? Why are you doing this? Are you so desperate for a man that you feel the need to settle for the first person who shows the slightest interest? That doesn't sound like you. The Merry I know is strong and knows she's strong. She doesn't need a man to make her happy. She's been through the fire before and has always come out on top." She paused for a moment. "I'm worried about you."

Meredith turned the steering wheel sharply and swerved off the road, gliding roughly onto the shoulder and sliding the gear into park. She held her head in her hands and cried.

"You must think I'm a wreck," she said, wiping her tears. "It seems I'm always having a crying fit when I'm talking to you."

"Since when are you self-conscious around me? Honey, you're falling apart. Do you need me to go down there? Please, just tell me what you need."

Meredith placed her elbows on the steering wheel and ran her fingers through her hair, pulling it back and closing her eyes. "I don't know anymore. I don't know which end is up. I just can't stand the suspense for one more day. Why does it always have to be so painful?"

"It doesn't have to be painful. When it's right, it won't be."

"It's been right three times!" Meredith exclaimed, throwing her hands in the air. "And every time, I allowed myself to feel safe. It only made it harder when it all crumbled around me. Tara, I can't do it again. I give up."

"Please don't give up. Just let me go down there and be with you for a day or two. We'll work this out together."

"No, you stay with your family this time. I hate that every time I have a problem you have to interrupt your life to deal with it. I'm sick of being a burden. I'm sick of crying. I'm done."

"Merry," Tara said, and Meredith detected tears in her voice. "Why are you saying such things? Have I ever given you the impression that I think you're a burden? I love you. I've always done my best to be there for you."

"I know you don't feel that way, but I do. Tara, I've got to get some control over my life. Enough is enough."

"But you're not taking control. Don't you see? You're grasping at straws. It's only the illusion of control. You think you're protecting yourself, but it's going to backfire in the end."

"It backfires every time. How many times do I have to get

burned before I'm justified in no longer caring? Will it be four? Five? Ten? That's too many times."

"I don't like Shane. He's not good to you. You're not happy with him, and I don't care how much you deny it."

"He's fun. He doesn't make me talk. He doesn't care what I do in my free time. And he likes to cook."

"He also doesn't ask you about your day, doesn't make sure you get into your car okay, doesn't care about your life, and has a family that treats you like shit. Where will you draw the line?"

Meredith straightened her shoulders to prepare to continue her drive home. "I draw the line at three times," she said, and eased back onto the road.

MEREDITH FELL into bed exhausted and ready to sink into oblivion. But oblivion she could not find. She spent the better part of an hour thinking about her life, as she had done so frequently as of late.

Meredith thought about Adam. She always came back to him, and she guessed she understood why. She had had perfection with Adam. She longed for that perfection once again. She saw other people enjoying it and wondered, *Why not me?* She had had it with Nick, but he had abandoned it. She could have had it with Wes, but he had clutched it too tightly. Adam hadn't been afraid, and he hadn't been impatient. She wondered where they would be today had he not passed away. She imagined their little auburn-haired children, and she wept bitterly.

She had come to the conclusion that perfection would not exist for her again. So why even try? Why not just accept it and move on? Who was to say what she should settle for and what she should fight for? With Nick and Wes she had fought for love and had lost it both times. Every time she loved, she ended up in pain. She thought again of Adam, of Nick, and of Wes. She thought even of the Bickharts, the loss of whom she still mourned, just as she mourned the loss of Wes. Maybe love wasn't in the cards for her. Maybe her real happiness would come from the peace of knowing she would never hurt from love again. Shane was fun, but if he left her tomorrow she wouldn't even care. She'd be sad that she would have to start over with somebody else, but it would be weariness, and not despair, that would weigh on her. The security of knowing she would never despair again was about as close to perfection as she could come.

She decided she didn't care that the Thayers didn't like her. Why should she concern herself with them? Even Shane didn't seem concerned with them. She doubted they'd have to see them much at all. And unlike the Bickharts, she had no attachment to the Thayers, which meant their disapproval meant little to her. She didn't know what was going to happen with Shane. But she intended to ride it out until its finish, for better or for worse. Part of her just didn't want to make any more decisions. The universe seemed hell bent on intervening just when things were looking good. Let the universe decide for her this time too. She dared the universe to hurt her again. She didn't think it could if it tried.

CHAPTER SIX

THINKING

*L*ife continued. April came to a conclusion, and May arrived. June would bring the school play. Meredith eagerly anticipated its performance; until then she had plenty to keep her busy. She was helping students write their term papers and trying to please Nancy by satisfying her many demands. She saw Katrina and Henry on Fridays after school. Shane usually drove down to take her to dinner on Saturday nights, and Sundays they'd go to lunch or see a movie. Their relationship had grown quite comfortable. Meredith genuinely enjoyed his company. He was funny, and he liked to have a good time. She liked that he didn't tell her what to do, or make decisions for her, something that could not be said for most other men in her life. She now cherished the fact that she never had to talk about her day. She needed the break. And she needn't worry about questioning him about his own day. She listened with interest to whatever he told her and commented appropriately, but he didn't even seem to care if she did or not. She found it refreshingly informal, or so she told herself.

During the week, Meredith taught her classes, after school sitting on her porch and grading papers, avoiding eye contact with the neighbors, except for Wes. Their relationship was cordial now, but they had had only a few more awkward conversations, not ready for an actual friendship just yet. Meredith couldn't help feeling some regret. She wondered what her life would be like at that moment had she simply accepted his proposal and married him right then, as he had wanted. She hated to admit it, but she knew she would be happy. When she had thoughts like these, it was all she could do to keep from going over there and telling him she had changed her mind.

One night, toward the middle of May, she and Shane had just returned from dinner and were sitting in his car, engaged in a passably exciting kiss. Shane had demonstrated a bit more rest-lessness as of late, and Meredith could sense he was growing frus-trated. So was she, but she preferred to endure it. She appreciated his refraining from pressuring her, but she knew it wouldn't be long before the issue would have to be addressed.

When she sensed him losing himself, his hands groping for her and his breath becoming more agitated, she stopped him. She had something important to tell him, and she didn't know how he would receive it. She knew this could be the end of their relation-ship, but it had to be said. If he left her right then, she would at least know she had done the right thing.

"Shane," she said, "I have to tell you something."

"Uh oh."

"It's nothing bad," she assured him. "Well, you might think it is. It's just that..." She hesitated for a moment, feeling silly saying these words but not having an alternative. "I've decided that I'm not having sex again until I get married. Or until I'm securely with a life partner, at least."

"Very funny."

She didn't say anything more, but bit her lip concernedly. He stared at her, his eyes widening.

"Oh—you mean, for real?"

"Yes, for real, Shane. I just can't. It's been too emotional an experience for me, and I'm not putting myself through it again until I'm sure I won't get hurt." She looked at him to discern his reaction. "I hope that's okay with you, but I'd understand if it isn't."

He was sitting very straight, looking at her attentively. Finally, when she was through speaking, he looked forward, out toward the front of the car. "Huh," he said. "Very interesting."

She was staring at him, bewildered by this emotionless reaction. "Is that all you have to say?"

He faced her again. "Well, if that's how you feel, I certainly can't change your mind." He furrowed his brow with thought. "That's cool, I guess. I understand."

Her eyes brightened. "You do?"

"Sure," he said, and smiled. "Hey," he continued, suddenly looking quite pleased. "Let's get married."

She looked at him with wide eyes, unsure of how to respond. She didn't know what he was talking about, whether he was joking or just not thinking. "What?"

"You heard me," he said, his smile widening.

"Wait—you're not kidding, are you!"

"Of course I'm not kidding! Why shouldn't we get married?" he asked, and lifted his hands toward the sky, as if it were the most obvious solution in the world. "You know, Meredith, you may not believe this, but I haven't had a whole lot of luck with women." Meredith suppressed a grin, not knowing whether he was serious. "I always pick the wrong women. They're never good for me. Well, I think you could be good for me." He smiled charmingly. "So what do you say? Will you marry me?"

Meredith couldn't stop staring at him. Her jaw had fallen, and her eyes were wide with shock. She couldn't believe he meant what he had suggested, but he certainly did not appear to be kidding around.

She had so many concerns. "What about your parents?"

"Screw my parents. I don't care. Let them tell people they're 'reaching across the aisle,' as politicos say. They'll get over it."

She considered this. "But we've only been dating for two months."

"So what? Look," he said, turning serious. He took her hand in his, a gentle gesture in which he rarely indulged. "We're still getting to know each other, right? That's okay. We don't have to know everything about each other. But I know you've been burned. Well, I've been burned too. I think we both know how much it hurts. So let's just put an end to it right now. We have fun together, right? We like each other, right? So come on. Let's just do it. Let's get married."

Meredith's mind was in a whirlwind of thought. Her heart was beating quickly, and she felt as if she couldn't breathe. And it wasn't because of Shane's proposal. It was because she had it in her head that she was going to do something, and she wanted to get out of the car and into her house right then so she could do it.

"Let me think about it," she told him abruptly. "I'll let you know tomorrow."

"Okay," he said. "That's fair."

She kissed him goodnight and hurried out of the car.

She stepped into her house and stood for several moments in the dark, not believing what she was about to do.

She didn't know what had possessed her to do it, but she knew it had to be done. She pulled her cell phone from her purse and stood right there by her front door, in the dark, and scrolled through her contacts for the number of a person she hadn't spoken to in over a year. Her heart was pounding so hard she couldn't hear herself think; she worried that she would faint right there on the spot and almost had to sit down from dizziness.

She dialed the number and felt the torment of panic as it rang. Suddenly she realized how late it was and worried that she would wake him.

"Hello?" said a quiet voice on the other end.

Meredith was breathing so heavily she almost couldn't speak. Her face was spread into an expression of shock. The sound of his voice brought everything back in a rush, and in an instant she felt that the world was good and beautiful again. She closed her eyes and imagined his handsome, angular face, imagined the feel of him against her and the way his blue eyes crinkled when he smiled. She thought of the pure, sincere love they had had together and of the pain she had felt for so many months when he had left, the pain she felt to this day.

"Hello," she said, but it was nearly a whisper. "Nick?"

"Merry?" he said, his voice bright with excitement and disbelief. "Is that you?"

"Yes," she said, and felt the tears ready to fall, but held them back. "Yes, it's me. How are you?"

"I'm good—I'm so happy to hear your voice," he said, his own voice more animated than she had ever heard it, save for during their emotional breakup. "It's just so good to hear your voice." He was almost breathless with relief.

Meredith thought her heart would shudder and break, it was so full. Instantly she felt she would be okay; she was taken back to a time when she had been optimistic, before the pain of the last year had had a chance to disillusion her. "It's good to hear your voice too," she said. "I—" She stopped. She wanted to tell him everything, that she had never fallen out of love with him, after all this time, even when she had fallen in love with someone else; that she had dreamed about him, had yearned for him even when she was sleeping; that she still could close her eyes and imagine the look of his face when he kissed her, the way his hands felt on her skin and the way his hair felt as it trickled through her fingers; that the days and nights they had spent together had been the best of her life; that with his gentleness, modesty, and sincerity he still represented to her the simple life she so desperately wanted, that she knew he was the only man in the world who could give it to her and that all she wanted was to live that life with him; and that he was beautiful in so many ways, so beautiful that she still cried when she thought of him, after more than a year.

She said, "I just had an undeniable urge to call you." She swallowed. "I've missed you."

"I've missed you too, beautiful—more than you know," he said, and Meredith closed her eyes once more and leaned against the door for support.

"So tell me how you've been," he said, settling in for a conversation. "Vince tells me you're living outside Washington now. Do you like it?"

"It's okay," she said, not wanting to talk about it at the moment. "It's been a rough year, but I'm fine. What about you?" she asked, wanting to hear his answer but more anxious to get to the point. "What have you been up to?"

"Actually, I've been working pretty hard. I'm doing a lot of jobs on the side, trying to make a little extra money. I don't like to travel that much anymore." He paused. "I think about you a lot."

Meredith was feeling more and more renewed with every passing moment. She was beginning to feel confident about what she was about to do. She sucked in her breath. "Nick," she said, "I'm calling you for a reason."

"Oh? What's that?"

"I have something to tell you." After a pause, she said, "Tonight a man asked me to marry him." She paused again. "I want you to tell me if I should."

There was dead silence on the other end. Meredith waited a long time for him to say something. She wanted him to tell her no, that she should not accept this proposal, that she should move up to Maine and marry him instead, that he hadn't gone a day without thinking of her and that he hadn't lost any love for her in all this time. If he told her he wanted her back, she would get in her car and drive up to see him right then, without a backward glance; he just needed to say the word, and she would go.

Meredith didn't know how much time had passed. But when

he spoke, he did not give her the answer she wanted to hear. He did not tell her he wanted her back; instead, he asked, "Do you want to marry him?"

Meredith could sense this conversation going downhill very quickly; she felt that if he didn't pick up on her desire right away, and act on it, that he wouldn't, but still she held out hope. "First I want you to tell me what you think I should do."

He was silent again, evidently unsure of what to say. "I can't tell you what to do," he said after several wordless moments. His voice sounded tense. "What do you want to do?"

I want to do whatever you want, was her answer, but she did not say it. Instead, she said, "What would you say if I told you I wanted to marry him?" In her heart she did not want to marry Shane, but she had to have the answer to this question.

Nick said nothing. Meredith waited and waited but did not get a response. Finally she prompted him.

"Well?"

After another moment or two of silence, Nick said, his voice low and flat, "Then I'd say I think you should marry him."

Meredith felt her heart breaking, disappointment and bitterness overwhelming her. She knew it would be only minutes before it morphed into the familiar anguish of despair. "You do?"

"Yes," he said, more adamantly, but his voice sounded hoarse. "I do."

"Do you want me to marry him?"

Nick paused this time for only a moment. "Yes, Merry," he said. "I want you to marry him."

Meredith swallowed but nearly choked; her throat was dry, and she was beginning to grow faint. "Okay then," she said shakily. "That's all I wanted to know." She closed her eyes again, breathing hard. "It was good to talk to you, Nick."

"It was good to talk to you too, Merry."

"Goodnight."

"Goodnight."

She hung up the phone.

MEREDITH WAS NOW PACING back and forth across her bedroom, not knowing what else to do with her energy. She was tired of sinking to the floor with misery; that was getting old. She needed to take action now. Now was the time to move on.

She was done with Nick. She had spent too many days and nights crying over him. She wondered why in hell she had let herself pine over him for so long when it was clear he was never coming back for her. She wondered if Wes has been right, if deep down she had rejected his proposal because of him, and she grew bitter. She didn't know how much happiness had been sacrificed mourning over Nick, but there would be no more.

Nick's rejecting her for the second time proved that love could only hurt her. She had extended her hand yet again, and yet again she had been disappointed. She wondered why she had bothered; she had learned that lesson by now and had been foolish to put herself out there once more.

She was never going to think of Nick again, and she was giving up on love for good this time.

She called Shane. He picked up on the first ring.

"Hey, babe. Don't tell me you have your answer already."

"Yes, I do. I'll marry you, Shane. Why not."

"Awesome!" he said. "That's great news!"

"Yes," she told him. "But I have one condition."

"What's that?"

"No long engagement. Let's get married right away." Meredith wanted to get this over as quickly as possible. No more waiting around. The sooner she was securely in a life she could plan and foresee, the happier she would be.

"Hey, that's fine with me—you took the words right out of my mouth!" he said, and Meredith hoped it wasn't because he knew she'd finally sleep with him once they were married, but she really didn't care. It was going to be over. No more uncertainty, no more pain. That was all that mattered now.

SHANE CALLED his parents the next day to inform them of his engagement to Meredith. He told her they had been silent for a long time, and then cold, and then had resigned themselves to the news, feeling slightly less despondent at Shane's suggestion that they use the engagement as a way for the senator to claim that he was reaching across the political aisle and that he was eager to make amends with the venerable journalist with whom he had quarreled in the past. Their engagement was announced in the newspaper and, among other claims, stated that the senator "hoped this blessed event would represent the overcoming of differences, both for the happiness of their families and for the betterment of the nation."

Meredith did not inform her family of her engagement right away, but she did tell her colleagues, who congratulated her without much warmth. Somehow, in spite of her efforts to exaggerate the advantages of her relationship with Shane and minimize the drawbacks, they had picked up on her desperation and had sensed that she was settling, and it had made them unhappy. However, they did not feel it was their place to intervene and had kept their opinions to themselves, figuring she knew best and that one never knew what went on behind closed doors—so who were they to judge?

Tara had been more forthright with her disapproval, telling Meredith over and over that she was making a big mistake and begging her to reconsider, threatening to drive down there and shake some sense into her if she refused to call off the engagement. She wasn't buying Meredith's praise of Shane, calling it "willful misrepresentation of the facts"—insisting, for instance, that what Meredith called his "letting her make her own decisions" was actually closer to complete lack of interest. She once again questioned Shane's motives, and she urged Meredith to consider his reliability as a partner, as the father of her children, and as an aspiring celebrity with long, unpredictable hours—all the practicalities of married life. Meredith told Tara she was welcome to visit but that her mind was made up, that she felt safer and calmer now than she had in a long time, that the security of knowing what the future held was preferable to a long, frightening wait that could very well end in the pain that was too familiar to her.

Meredith and Shane got engaged on Saturday; on Wednesday, the announcement appeared in the newspaper, stating that a June wedding was planned, as the happy couple sought to begin their life together as soon as possible. That evening Meredith was just finishing dinner when she was startled by furious banging on her front door. Cautiously she stepped out of the kitchen and toward the front of the house, where she peeked outside to ascertain who it was, though she had a feeling she already knew. Wes was standing outside her door, wearing his usual jeans, t-shirt, and collared shirt, unbuttoned with the sleeves rolled up. He had begun banging the door again, more loudly than before, his hand balled into a tight fist.

She waited for the banging to stop, then opened the door. Wes's face, which usually displayed confidence and good humor, was contorted into an expression of fury. She had seen his face clouded by suffering over the last couple of months, but he had managed to hold himself together. All attempts at a show had now been forgotten, all ability to conceal his anguish now vanished.

He was staring at her, his lips taut and his eyes wide, his arms at his sides and his entire body tight with stress.

"You're engaged?" he bellowed at her. "You're going to marry him? After you put me through hell, strung me along for months without giving me an answer, after you left me alone with a house and a ring—you're going to marry Shane Thayer after two months?"

Meredith felt nauseated and for a moment believed she would be sick. She stepped backward into the house, away from him, and wrapped her arms around herself, the only protection she could think of.

"How did you find out?" she asked weakly.

Wes strode in after her and slammed the door. "It's in the fucking paper, Meredith!" He held up his hand. For the first time Meredith noticed he was holding a newspaper. It was still open to the engagement announcement. He appeared to have wasted no time in confronting her after reading it.

"Oh," she uttered, flustered.

"You're going to need to do better than that," he spat angrily, pointing his finger at her. "I want an explanation for this. I want you to tell me why. I deserve at least that much."

Meredith didn't know what to say. She knew how much he was hurting and that he had a right to be hurt. If she were in his shoes she'd feel exactly the same way. She was mad at herself on his behalf. But she felt numb. She wanted to feel sympathy for Wes, knew that she should and that deep down she did, but her defenses were up, and she was protecting herself. At least she was able to think clearly.

She could only tell him the truth. "Yes, it's true," she said, unnecessarily. "I'm engaged. I'm sorry, Wes. I know this must be hard for you."

He raised his eyebrows with disbelief, then scrunched up his face with disgust. "Is that all you have to say to me?" he asked, his voice strained now, as he grew more and more shocked and more and more angry. "We had the real thing, Meredith. I thought we loved each other. I thought we were happy. I thought we were going to be together, damn it!" Here he threw the paper across the room; it fluttered softly, anti-climactically, to the ground.

"How could you do this? How could you leave me, only to marry Shane? You must be out of your damn mind!" He threw his hands into the air and shook his head. "You know," he said, placing his hands on his hips and hanging his head low. He lifted his head and looked at her. "I tried to see it from your point of view. I tried to understand why you would give up what we had, and the life we could have had. I know how I can be, Meredith. You're not the first person to tell me." His expression became pained, and Meredith's heart ached for him. "I told you before that I think you made a big mistake. I think you were unwise to give it all up. Nobody's perfect. I would have given you the world if you had just forgiven me my flaws. But you couldn't tolerate them, and I have to accept that." He put his hands up, the gesture suggesting that he was giving her that point, but begrudgingly. "But this," he said, and bent over to retrieve the newspaper, and shook it in her face. "This is more than I can bear. This is beyond insulting, and beyond stupid. What the hell are you thinking, Meredith? Are you going to stand there and tell me that the prospect of a life with him is acceptable, but of a life with me is not? Do you really think you can be happier with him than you could have been with me?"

"No," Meredith said, holding her hand to her heart and looking him straight in the eye. Tears of fury pricked her eyes, but she yelled through them. "I don't."

"Then what's the problem?" he shouted, throwing his hands in the air once more, the paper rustling in his hand. "Listen, Meredith," he said then, his voice now tense and low. He leaned forward so his face was close to hers, and he watched her carefully as he spoke. "I love you. I never stopped loving you. Shane doesn't love you, and he never will. I'd like to know how you rationalize that."

"I love you too, Wes, and that's the problem, don't you see? I can't do it anymore. I just can't get hurt again, and as much as you love me, you'll hurt me again."

"You know the last thing in the world I want to do is hurt you. How can you say that?"

"Because nothing ever changes. I told you and told you what I needed from you—and the one thing I needed was always the one thing you couldn't give me. I don't care about your house or your ring. Those are things you thought I needed. And you completely ignored me in the process of giving them to me. If you had been paying any attention at all you would have seen that what I needed was for you to listen, really listen, and to make a life together, not the one you had planned for yourself and by yourself."

He frowned. "And Shane? Does he listen?"

"No, but I don't care. He requires nothing from me, nor I from him."

"But you don't love him!"

"No love means no pain."

Wes shook his head again, his expression softening. "Oh, sweetheart," he said, his voice more gentle now. "I can't stand to watch you do this. I can't stand to think of you spending your life in a loveless marriage when you could be with me instead. When I imagine you together, his hands on you—" He closed his eyes and shook his head. When he opened his eyes again, his expression was severe. He said, "Don't do this. I know you, Meredith, and I know this isn't what you want. It's bad enough that you gave up on us when the going got tough. Don't give up on your life too, and end any chance you'll ever have for happiness."

Meredith had been inclined to sympathize with him until he said these words, and she once again bristled at the suggestion that the failure of their relationship was entirely her fault. Stiffening, she said, "You've just shown that you actually don't know me at all. Please leave my house, and let me be. You've made clear how you feel, not that I asked for your opinion. I don't enjoy being yelled at, and I sure as hell don't enjoy being blamed for all of your misery. Now get out, and don't talk to me again until you're ready to really hear me."

Wes pursed his lips tautly as he made every effort to control his fury. "Fine," he said through clenched teeth, turning toward the door. "Just don't blame me when your life goes to hell." With that, he opened the door and stalked out, slamming it with a bang.

Meredith went to the door and peeked out through the window, watching him as he walked across the street. He was striding with long, quick steps, his shirt billowing behind his back. When he reached his lawn, he bent over, without slowing his pace, and picked up a rock, which he threw violently against the foundation of his house. He continued toward the porch until, skipping several steps, he reached his front door and stormed inside, not to be seen again for the rest of the night.

MEREDITH'S NIGHT became even worse when her phone rang not a half hour later. She glanced wearily at the screen. When she saw who it was, she closed her eyes and sighed. She was tempted not to answer it, but she knew she was going to have to deal with it sooner or later and figured now was as good a time as any, while she already was in a rotten mood. She braced herself and answered the phone.

"Hi, Dad," she said, trying to make her voice chipper.

"Hello, Meredith," said Harold Beck. "Guess what I just heard. I'll give you a hint. It involves you."

"I suppose you're referring to my engagement to Shane Thayer," Meredith said, her head in her hand.

"Good guess. When were you planning on telling us about this?"

"I was going to call you this week."

"I think I can figure out why you hesitated. This is the worst news I've heard in a long time. I almost had a heart attack when I found out. I told your mother this must be some kind of sick joke. How long have you two been dating?"

"About two months."

There was silence. "Two months," said Harold, and paused. "Meredith, what's going on?"

"What do you mean?" she asked, suddenly angry. Why did everyone ask her what was going on? The people in her life acted like nobody ever got engaged. Nobody knew her reasons for marrying Shane, and it was none of anybody's business.

"You're usually not this senseless," said her father. "Your good sense is the one thing you've got going for you. Where the hell is it right now? What are you thinking?"

That was another question everyone had been asking her, and it was starting to get on her nerves. Why did everyone assume the right to know her thoughts? Nobody understood what she was going through, not her father, not Wes, not even Tara. Her experiences were unique to herself, and she was sick of being told what to do.

"How do you know what I'm doing is senseless? You don't know anything about the situation. You didn't even know I was dating Shane. Maybe you should start by assuming I have good reasons rather than by assuming I don't."

Meredith's father said nothing for several tense moments. "Okay," he said then. "I'll do as you ask, and I'll assume you have good reasons. Please tell me what they are."

Meredith knew what she thought were good reasons would sound absurd to her father. She couldn't tell him the truth. "I'm in love with him," she said, her voice unconvincingly monotone.

"Don't insult me," said Harold. "Believe it or not, I happen to know a little bit about Shane Thayer. The man's a punk. He has a history of failure and of womanizing, and the only reason he's made it as far as he has is that his domineering parents have intervened on his behalf. He's going nowhere, and fast, and if you have any self-respect at all you'll end this before it gets any further."

"I'm not ending it, Dad," Meredith declared, though he had scared her a little with his comments about Shane. She would ask Shane about them later. For now she had to deal with her father. "Are you going to walk me down the aisle?"

Harold again said nothing. "I don't know, Meredith," he said finally. "You've put me in a very uncomfortable position. I just don't get it." He paused again. Meredith could almost hear him trying to figure this out. "Shane Thayer, of all people, Meredith. Are you doing this because he's attractive? Are you pregnant?" he asked suddenly, his voice taking on a loud, accusatory tone.

"No, God, no!" Meredith cried. "Why would you even ask me that?"

"There just has to be a reason for this nonsense. Shane Thayer, for chrissake! John Thayer's good-for-nothing son. Is that it? Are you trying to hurt me, Meredith?"

"This isn't about anybody but me," she said, her voice cold and calm. She was about to end this phone call and was having her final say. From now on she was defending herself to no one. "I want to marry him. It's none of your business why. Now, you can either support me by attending the wedding next month, or you can choose not to. It's up to you. But the wedding is happening whether you like it or not. This conversation is over."

"Now, look here, Meredith—"

"Goodbye, Dad," she said, and pulled the phone from her face, ready to hang up. But before she did, she held it back to her lips for one more brief moment. "I love you," she said tersely. Then she hung up.

MEREDITH SAT where she was at the kitchen island, her elbow leaning on the table, her hand cupping her chin. She absentmindedly flipped her phone over and over in her hand and against the countertop, oblivious to the sound it made. She was thinking very hard.

None of her reasons for marrying Shane had changed. She was glad to have an end in sight, to know what the future would bring. She still thought Shane was a good compromise; he was fun, and he kept her company, but her feelings for him weren't strong enough to put her in any danger.

On the other hand, everyone she knew thought this was a bad idea. Maybe she should listen to them; maybe her friends and family had a point. She knew she wasn't thinking all that clearly, that she was acting on emotion. Reluctantly she considered that maybe she was making a big mistake.

But then she thought about the people who had told her so, and she felt again that she was right. Nobody knew what she had been through. Katrina, Henry, and Scott all were in happy, serious, long-term relationships, with bright futures ahead of them. Tara, as much as Meredith loved her, couldn't relate; she had been married for years and had two beautiful children. Wes's motives were obviously biased. And her father didn't know her at all. He had never even heard of Nick or of Wes. In short, nobody who had told her not to marry Shane had any idea the kind of pain she had experienced in such a short time. She thought with bitterness that if they had, perhaps they wouldn't be in such a rush to criticize her.

Meredith felt completely and utterly alone, with no one she could talk to who would understand what she was going through. She couldn't remember the last time she had felt that she was so close to rock bottom.

Her phone rang again. She was afraid to know who it was. When she glanced at the screen, she grinned, feeling a mixture of happiness and amusement.

"Hey," she said when she answered the phone. "Did Dad tell you to call me?"

"Yes," said Vince on the other end. "He said you're engaged to Chef Shane Thayer. What the hell?"

"I'm sorry, Vince. I forgot to mention I was dating Shane. It's only been a couple of months."

"I know you've got a lot going on, Merry, but how can you 'forget' to tell me that? Are you—"

"If you ask me if I'm okay, or what I'm thinking, I will hang up this phone right now."

"Damn, Merry. I was going to ask if you were drunk, but as long as you mentioned it, I am kind of wondering what the story is here. You don't sound quite right. How did you meet the chef? When did you get engaged? Why are you marrying him? What is going on here?"

"I met him at his restaurant a couple of months ago. We've been seeing each other since, and we have fun together. We got engaged last week, and I'm marrying him because I want to. There's really not much more to tell than that."

"If you say so," Vince said. "Funny how you ended up meeting him again. What a small world."

"Yes, it is. You should come down and see me sometime, and you can meet him."

"I'm two steps ahead of you. I'm coming down to see you this weekend."

"What?"

"Dad wants me to go down there and talk some sense into you. But he wants me to do it without pissing you off. He told me you're acting irrationally and that you yelled at him, and that it's clear that you're doing this just because he's telling you not to."

"Dad gives himself way too much credit," Meredith sneered. "He must be desperate if he's sending you down to talk to me about relationships."

"Tell me about it. He's even paying for my ticket."

"You're flying?"

"I'm in Chicago."

"Is Nick with you?"

"No. Why?"

"I'm just curious."

Meredith waited, but Vince said no more about Nick. Meredith breathed a sigh of relief; evidently Nick had not told Vince that she had called.

She spent another few minutes on the phone with her brother while they investigated flights. After a call to Shane, it was decided that Shane would pick Vince up from the airport on Friday while Meredith was at school and drive him to her house that evening. That way they all could have dinner together, and Vince wouldn't have to take a car or wait until Meredith arrived home to fly into town. Meredith was pleased that Shane had so readily agreed to this plan and to making the effort to alter his schedule, and thanked him, hanging up feeling warmly toward him. She called her brother back and chatted with him for another few minutes before turning in for the night.

But before she did, she spent an hour reading about Shane online. She had looked him up before but had not taken her research too seriously. She wanted to pay special attention to anything that would support her father's claim that Shane was a notorious womanizer. She saw photos of him with several women and read a couple of articles in which it was suggested that he had yet to settle down, but she found nothing to indicate that she had anything to worry about. He seemed to have been searching, and nothing more, just as she had. She wondered what her love life would look like, how it would be interpreted, if it were sprawled across the internet for all to see, and she sneered. It probably wouldn't look very impressive at all.

CHAPTER SEVEN

BEST FRIENDS

riday afternoon Meredith arrived home from work, sad to miss dinner with Henry and Katrina but excited to see her brother. She also was nervous for him to meet Shane. Shane's moods were rather unpredictable, and she didn't know how Vince would receive him. She hoped the two would like each other and was eager to see them interact together. Meredith had given Shane Wes's key, which she had humbly knocked on Wes's door to ask him for, and had thought he and Vince could get acquainted until she came home.

But she was disappointed when she pulled into her driveway to find that they hadn't yet arrived. She looked at the clock. It was after five o'clock. Vince's flight was supposed to land at one o'clock, which by Meredith's calculations meant that he and Shane should have been home by around three o'clock. She figured Vince's flight had been delayed and went inside to try to complete some schoolwork before her busy weekend. She didn't cook dinner, as the three of them had planned to go out.

At seven o'clock her phone rang, and she eagerly grabbed it from the table. It was Shane.

"Hey, babe," he said, his voice bright and upbeat. "Sorry we're running late. I just wanted to check in."

"Oh," Meredith said, and smiled. "Thanks. Was Vince's flight delayed?"

"No, it was here on time. He and I decided to hang out a little as long as you weren't home yet, but we lost track of time. We're on our way to your place right now."

"You and my brother hung out without me?"

"Yeah. I love your brother! Why haven't you had him down to see you before?"

"I don't know," she said absentmindedly, not knowing what to make of all this.

"Well, we'll see you in a few. It'll be too late to go out to dinner, but I'll make something when we get there. Okay?"

"Okay."

"Cool. Later!"

He hung up.

An hour later she heard the key in the door and jumped up to meet them. Shane entered first, looking suave and handsome in a black jacket and t-shirt, with dark jeans; he kissed her lightly on the lips before stepping aside so Meredith could greet Vince, who was dressed similarly to Shane. He opened his arms wide to receive her, and she held him for a long time before letting go; she hadn't realized how much she had missed him.

She pulled away and looked at him, and sighed with relief. "I'm so happy to see you, Vince," she told him, and rubbed his arm affectionately. "Thank you for coming."

Vince studied her, his face more serious than she was used to. "I'm happy to see you too. I'm really glad to be here."

Something about his tone made Meredith look at him more carefully. He was trying to act nonchalant, but he wasn't doing a very good job. She asked him to tell her about their evening as Shane strode into the kitchen and opened her refrigerator, contemplating the contents and grabbing an item here and there.

They followed him, and Meredith let him take control of her kitchen as she and her brother sat on the bar stools and chatted.

"Shane is quite a guy," Vince said. "He took me to several new hot spots in DC. He knows them all."

"I was happy to do it," Shane said as he pulled a bag of asparagus out of the refrigerator. "I'm always up for an afternoon on the town. Meredith, you don't have any fontina, do you?"

"No."

"That's okay. The gruyere will do."

Meredith turned back to Vince and resumed her questioning. "So what did you do?"

"We grabbed a bite to eat. Walked around. You know. The usual."

Vince's voice was curt, and Meredith watched him to try to determine what was going on. He reached for the fruit bowl and grabbed an apple, and took a swift bite. He chewed loudly as she stared at him.

"Do you ever talk to Sandy?" Meredith asked.

Vince nearly choked on his apple. After a moment, he swallowed. "No. Who's Sandy?" he smirked, and took another bite.

"Cool painting," said Shane, gesturing toward Vince's watercolor as he cut the asparagus. "I like the dark colors."

Meredith smiled. "I'm so glad you noticed that. Vince painted it," she said, patting her brother's arm. "He's really a gifted painter."

"You paint, man? That's awesome. I wouldn't have guessed."

Vince swallowed a bite of apple and shrugged, turning his glass on the counter mindlessly. "I used to paint. I really don't anymore."

"That's like me and piano. My mother nags me about it, tells me I'm wasting my talent or whatever." He tossed a pile of chopped asparagus into a bowl, his large hands easily containing the pieces. "Can't do everything."

Vince said nothing; he was staring at the countertop, seemingly deep in thought.

Conscious of the tension, Meredith changed the subject. She and Vince chatted while Shane made dinner, concentrating fully on what he was doing and rarely interjecting. When it was finished, he dished out three plates of asparagus lasagna, handing one to Meredith and Vince and keeping the third for himself. He ate standing up, leaning against the countertop, while the other two sat.

"Hey, this is great," said Vince between bites. "I'm impressed."

"Yes, it's fantastic," Meredith agreed.

Shane did not respond. He was cleaning the remainder of the dishes, absorbed in his own thoughts.

Vince said, "Merry, why is it that all your boyfriends cook dinner for me? You must have them wrapped around your finger."

At these words, Shane looked up. "What are you talking about?"

"Wes cooked for us, too, the last time Vince was in town," Meredith explained.

Shane's face darkened. "So the golden boy can cook, too. Why am I not surprised?"

Meredith stared at him with a frown of disapproval. "Please don't call him that."

Shane popped a stray piece of asparagus into his mouth and held up his hands. "Sorry."

Vince was taking a long swig from his glass of water and was silent.

"Well," Shane said, looking around the kitchen with his hands on his hips, satisfied with the cleanliness, "I guess I'd better get out of here. It's pretty late. Are we hanging out tomorrow?"

"Sure," Meredith said. "What should we do?"

"How about you and Vince come by my place? I'll make lunch. Then we'll go out."

"Okay," said Meredith. She hadn't even seen Shane's house yet. "That sounds like fun."

"Alrighty then," Shane exclaimed, rubbing his hands together and smiling. "I'm out. Good to meet you, Vince." He extended his hand. "It was a blast."

"You too," Vince replied as he took it; the two men shook hands and clapped each other on the back. "Thanks for dinner."

"Night, babe," Shane said to Meredith, and kissed her. He grabbed his keys from the table in the hallway and opened the door. "See you tomorrow." He walked out, closing the door brusquely as he left.

Meredith turned to Vince. "Well? What do you think?"

Vince didn't look at her for a moment; he was staring at the door. Finally his gaze met hers. "Do you want my honest opinion?"

Meredith instantly felt her heart sink as she sensed she was going to receive the same dour opinion as she had from everyone else. "Go ahead," she said dejectedly, with a sigh.

"I don't like him, Merry. I'm sorry, but it's how I feel."

"What's the matter with him?"

"I can't put my finger on it," Vince said, looking back at the door and frowning.

"That doesn't sound very definite to me."

Vince turned to her. "All right, Merry. You want to know the truth? I'll tell you." He took a deep breath and squared his shoulders. "I don't trust him. I don't like the way he wanted to hang out in DC today without you. I don't like the way he seems to want to be my best friend. He's too into partying. I didn't like the way he acted while we were out."

Meredith frowned. "Why? What did he do?"

"Nothing. He didn't do anything you'd disapprove of." He shifted his weight. "But I think he would have if he had been with someone other than your brother."

"Well, you can't know that for sure, though. Is there anything else, that you know for sure?"

Vince studied her, his face stern. Suddenly his expression softened. "Why are you defending him, Merry? What's so special about Shane, anyway? He doesn't seem anything like the kind of guy you'd usually go for. How do you go from Wes to Shane? Why are you marrying Shane and not Wes? That's what I don't understand."

"You don't have to understand it," Meredith said angrily, feeling the familiar burn of tears. "All you have to do is support me. Why is that so hard for you to do?"

"I want to support you. That's why I'm telling you the truth. You know how much I hate to agree with Dad, but in this case I have to. I really think you'd be making a mistake to marry Shane. He's too much like—" Vince's face turned white, and he stopped short.

"He's too much like what?"

"Nothing. Forget it."

He and Meredith stared at each other in silence.

After a moment, Meredith said, "You know, Vince, I'm getting a little tired of the way you always intervene in my relationships. It's almost like you don't even want me to be happy."

"What are you talking about?"

"You told me you didn't want me with Nick either. You spent weeks giving us the cold shoulder, and you called me a slut."

"Merry, please don't go there. I told you I was sorry."

"Don't be sorry; just don't do it. Don't tell me how to run my life. I just wish everyone would stop telling me how to run my life! Everyone knows better than I do what's best for me! I'm tired of it!"

"Meredith, what has gotten into you? You're totally out of control!"

"Well, at what point am I allowed to say it's enough? At what point do I have the right to just take control of my own life? When will people stop imposing their opinions and allow me to make my own decisions? You're not going to do this again, Vince. You're not going to sabotage my relationship with Shane. You almost ruined my relationship with Nick—not that it needed any help falling apart."

"Listen, Merry. I've been meaning to bring that up. What I said about you and Nick—"

"No!" Meredith screamed, the tears now blurring her vision of him. "I don't want to hear it! You've said quite enough already."

"Meredith, please, listen to me. Nick—"

"Nick nothing. Leave me alone. Goodnight."

She stalked upstairs and into her bedroom, and slammed the door.

THE NEXT MORNING, Meredith attempted to pretend she and Vince had not quarreled the night before, but she was too upset to avoid sulking. She was concerned by the fact that she never seemed to be at ease anymore; she was constantly tense, and she had little patience for anybody. This made her downcast and irritable, and she knew it, and didn't like it. She dismissed her mood as the result of nerves and assured herself that once she and Shane were married and she had some kind of stability in her life, she would go back to her usual positive self. In the meantime, she would try her best to put on a happy face and go about business as cheerfully as she could.

Vince followed her lead and didn't reference their argument, but he too seemed pensive and ill-humored. Several times she cast her gaze in his direction only to find him staring ruefully at her, at which point he would look downward with a frown or attempt a weak smile that was almost more grim. He appeared always on the verge of saying something, but he spoke little, and Meredith didn't push him. If it was that important, he would say it. If not, she was just as happy not to be subjected to another lecture.

They made the trip out to Shane's house in awkward silence, each of them trying to stir up conversation but failing, receiving short, unenthusiastic answers in return. Meredith wondered why they didn't seem to be getting along this time around. Even their fight shouldn't have put this much tension between them. She thought with sorrow as she drove that she truly was alone.

Shane's townhouse looked nearly identical to his sister's. It was in an upscale community with impressive landscaping and neatly tailored lawns, expensive cars in all the driveways. Meredith parked, and she and Vince climbed out of the car without saying a word. But as they approached Shane's door, Vince stopped Meredith by placing his hand on her arm and holding her back.

"Hey," he said. "I want to support you. You have good judgment. I trust you. Whatever you need from me, I'll give you." He swallowed. "Okay?"

Meredith looked at him for a moment. "Okay. Thanks."

Vince placed his hand on her shoulder and escorted her up to Shane's door.

It took Shane a long time to answer the door, but when he did, his eyes were bright with enthusiasm. "Hey!" He greeted them with a wide smile. "Glad you made it." He shook Vince's hand, then brought Meredith in for a firm kiss right on the lips.

"I've been thinking about you," he said, a soft lilt in his voice. His eyes bore into hers. "You look really pretty today."

Meredith smiled, surprised and delighted. "Thanks," she said, blushing, and looked down at herself. She was wearing jeans and a pink t-shirt with a wide neck, and her hair was in a ponytail. She didn't think it was anything special.

Shane had lunch all ready—Waldorf chicken salad with home-made rolls, and a spring fruit salad. They ate at a modern dark wood table, finding little things to say here and there but largely remaining quiet.

Meredith missed Wes. She was trying to convince herself that the frequent lulls in the conversation that were normal for her and Shane were preferable to the necessity for small talk, but with a frown she remembered that with Wes there never was any small talk. They had so much to say to each other that they had often lost track of time, talking well into the night and suffering from exhaustion the next day. Wes was smart, interesting, and witty; Meredith had relished their conversations and always felt brighter after having them. And for as much as Wes had wanted to dictate the circumstances of her life, he always respected her during their discussions, admiring her for her sharp opinions and letting her have her say.

No longer hungry, Meredith pushed her food around on her plate and let the sadness take over her face. Worse than any breakup was the change that had overcome her. She wasn't used to wallowing in misery. She always had managed to put on a smile and move on, even through her tears; her strength had guided her through heartache. She didn't know what was so different now or why it was occurring at this point in her life. She wondered if it was her breakup with Wes, or her conversation with Nick, or her being at odds with everyone else she knew in the world, or a culmination of all three, that was bringing her down, holding her under this cloud of despair. She wanted desperately to get out of it but didn't know how.

She looked up at Shane. He and Vince were talking about sports. Meredith asked herself how she felt about this man being her primary support system, every day for the rest of her life. She asked herself if she would rather be alone than get her hopes up about Shane and be disappointed. She knew he wasn't capable of being the rock she needed him to be. As husbands went, he would be the least desirable of all the loves of her life. She asked herself if she was willing to accept that, and for a second she questioned what she was doing, how she could settle like this. She had to consciously recall why she was marrying him at all.

Then she remembered Nick's voice, how she had felt when he had told her to marry Shane, that he wanted her to marry Shane. She thought about the year she had spent mourning Nick, never losing hope that he would come back to her. The possibility that one day the story would conclude with a happy ending was what had kept her going. But now there was no hope. For a moment she considered going back to Wes. Then she thought of him telling her that she had given up on them, and she put that idea out of her head.

She asked where the restroom was and excused herself, hurrying from the table so she could wash her face and regroup before rejoining the men. She needed to talk to Shane. She needed him to remind her of why he was a better option than no man at all.

SHANE TOLD them he was going to surprise them and take them someplace special. The three of them piled into his car and took off, Shane driving too fast down the highway. When he pulled into a parking lot, Meredith saw that he was taking them to play miniature golf. She turned to him, confused.

He looked around and held up his hands. "It's a beautiful day. I'm with two people I really like. We're off from work, and we don't have to think about anything." He smiled. "Do you have something against miniature golf?"

"No."

"Good. I was thinking for a minute that this wasn't going to work out."

Meredith wished it were that easy. She followed Shane and Vince into the park, for the first time noticing how similar they were in appearance. Shane by far was brawnier, making her already brawny brother look positively puny by comparison, but they walked with the same calm confidence and spoke with the same playful enthusiasm.

They didn't seem to notice that she spent much of her time trailing behind, deep in thought. She played the game quietly, letting them do all the talking, following them when they walked and stopping when they stopped, trying to enjoy the nice weather and the peaceful atmosphere around her, noticing out of the corner of her eye the happy families and loving couples that strode leisurely through the park together, grateful to be spending time together.

They finished their game and turned in their clubs and balls. Meredith thought it was now or never.

"Vince," she said, turning to her brother, "would you mind giving me a minute to talk to Shane?"

"Sure," he said, and patted her shoulder. Shane tossed him the keys, and Vince walked toward the car alone.

"What's up?" Shane asked, looking down at her expectantly, his hands in his pockets.

"Shane," she said, forcing herself to make her voice steady, "I've been doing a lot of thinking. I just don't know if we're doing the smartest thing here. I think maybe we rushed into this engagement."

Shane's eyes widened, and his face took on a concerned look. "What? Why?"

Meredith watched him carefully. "Are you telling me that you can't understand why I might think we're moving too quickly? I mean, we barely even know each other. We're so different. And—"

"Meredith," Shane interrupted, and held her shoulders in his hands. "Just relax. You're so stressed out it's giving me a headache." He removed his hands and put them back in his pockets. "Of course I understand what you're saying. But I just don't care about any of that. At least, not anymore. Do you know how many women I've been with?"

Meredith didn't answer, not knowing what she was supposed to say.

"Well, let me tell you: it's a lot. I know I shouldn't be saying that, but you're not stupid, and I'm not going to lie. And that's just the point, Meredith—you're not stupid. I'm so used to being with the same woman, over and over, the kind of woman who just wants to see where I'm going, maybe thinks she'll end up in a magazine or something, looks at me as some dumb trophy to have a good time with. I'm sick of those women. They're all the same."

Meredith continued to watch him, intrigued.

"Then I met you, and you told me I couldn't cook worth a damn." He laughed and folded his arms across his chest. "I wondered what it would be like to be with someone with a brain. I kind of like it. It feels good to know I can say something to you and you'll actually understand what the hell I'm talking about."

"Shane—"

"No, let me finish," he said, and put his hands on her shoulders once more. His voice turned softer than she had ever heard it before. "Listen," he told her, his hands moving up and down her arms. "I know it's kind of strange. I know *I'm* kind of strange. I know we're different and that we haven't had enough time to figure this thing out. But the thing is, Meredith," he began, and hesitated. After thinking for a few moments, he said, "The thing is that I don't know how to do this. I'm hoping as we know each other longer, I'll figure it out, that you can show me how. So far you've seemed willing to try." He had been looking at her shoulders as his hands caressed them; at these words, his gaze shifted to her eyes, his eyebrows raised imploringly. "Maybe I'm wrong about us. But in the meantime, we have fun, right? So why don't we just go for it, and give it a try? Will you, please? Come on. What's the worst that could happen?"

Meredith thought about the worst that could happen. She

didn't know if she wanted to fall in love with Shane or if she wanted to avoid falling in love with him. But his words had moved her. She was pleased that he had opened up to her, that he seemed willing to see it from her point of view and that he actually did have reasons for wanting to marry her. She had been wondering what had drawn him to her. Now she was beginning to understand.

She had spent years following her heart, and it had brought her nothing but misery. Three times she had entered relationships with men she knew she would fall in love with. Obviously she needed a change. The right man always seemed to lead her down the wrong path. Maybe this time the wrong man would lead her down the right path.

"Okay," she said, and smiled. "Let's do it. Let's get married."

Shane hugged her and clapped her on the back as he led her to the car, his arm around her waist. As they approached, Meredith sought her brother's face. He was sitting in the backseat, watching them. He was frowning, his entire face, from brow to lips, turned downward, his expression one of disappointment, fear, and hopelessness.

SUNDAY MORNING, Meredith drove her brother to the airport. They had a somber goodbye, Vince holding her and telling her he'd see her at the wedding, but not sounding pleased about it. Meredith kissed him goodbye and thanked him for coming down to see her. With a smirk he told her he'd have to give their father the bad news and that she owed him one. She punched his shoulder playfully and told him he could cash in the favor any time.

As she drove back home, Meredith tried to look at the situation objectively. She had no hard evidence of any wrongdoing on Shane's part. Until she did, she would assume they could be passably happy together. She thought about what it would take for her to break up with Shane. The formal engagement announcement already had been made. They had passed the awkward beginning stages of relationships when people first get to know each other and aren't comfortable in normal conversation. If she broke up with him, she'd have to do all that again with somebody new, somebody she couldn't even guarantee would be a good companion for her.

She decided she was too far in. At this point, the effort of breaking up with Shane would be greater than the effort of marrying him. It was a matter of practicality, really.

MEREDITH WAS WALKING in an open field under the stars. She couldn't see much of her surroundings; it was all a vague haze. But she saw the man walking beside her, and she smiled. His face was blurry, and she couldn't determine his features, but she could see that he was tall, blond, and handsome. She felt safe and warm in his presence, and she held out her hand to him. He took it and returned her smile.

"I love you," he said.

Suddenly she was turning her head to look over her shoulder and calling a name she couldn't quite hear. A little blond child ran to her and stood beside her. She ruffled the child's hair and sent him on his way. Before running off, the child jumped into the arms of the man next to her; the man kissed the child a hundred times, eliciting giggles from the child, before placing him back down on the ground and watching as he scampered off to play.

The man was leaning in to kiss her. She met him halfway and sighed as their lips touched.

Abruptly she pulled away, remembering that she was engaged.

"Should I marry him?" she asked.

"No," he said. "Don't marry him. Marry me."

CHAPTER EIGHT

GOOD TIMES

The following weekend she was going to spend at the Thayers' house to help settle some details for the wedding, which would take place right after graduation toward the end of June, and also to celebrate Tess's birthday. Meredith had let the Thayers book their country club for the wedding, not wanting to fight that battle with them and not really caring where the wedding was held. Truth be told, she didn't care about anything but her dress, and she would have let Tess and Maribel do all the planning had she not been afraid that her passivity would give them the impression that she intended to sit by and let them make decisions for her in the future. So she agreed to spend the weekend with the Thayers, grateful that Shane had agreed to stay there, as well—in a separate bedroom, of course.

Meredith had braced herself and called Tess, thanking her in advance for her hospitality and asking permission to cook her a special birthday dinner. Tess had been silent for several moments after this request but had told Meredith that it was a lovely idea and that she would have Shane send her the recipes she would like prepared on her birthday. There were four recipes, all of them traditional to the family, having been passed down for generations. Meredith had planned to use this opportunity to finally attempt pâté en croûte—she wanted to put forth her best and greatest effort, not only to impress Tess but also to prove how eager she was to please her. However, she certainly did not want to argue with her about it. Once again putting aside her desire to conquer the pâté en croûte, she said she would be delighted to cook these special dishes, and she hung up the phone hopeful that she would be able to put the tension behind them once and for all.

Shane emailed her the recipes. Meredith eagerly looked them over, confident that she could prepare all of them to Tess's liking, except one.

She read the crab cake recipe and frowned. "Blue-tip basil?" she mumbled, worried. She had never heard of this before. She called Shane.

"Very few growers cultivate it," he told her. "It was invented by a Maryland farmer, and not everyone knows about it. It has a sweeter taste than other basils."

"Will I be able to find it?"

"You should. I'll give you a few names, but you'll need to start calling them now."

"What if I can't? What's a good substitute?

"Oh, you don't want to go there, babe," Shane told her, his voice grave. "These are family recipes. There are no substitutes. Just make sure you find it."

Meredith nervously called the three farms Shane had recommended. Only one farm had it: it was in Tillytown, Maryland, nearly a two-hour drive from Lovelace. Relieved, she told the farmer she would be there Thursday evening to pick it up, to be ready to bring it to Frederick on Friday evening. She gathered some other ingredients and prepared a few things in advance. The dinner would take place on Sunday night.

Thursday afternoon, she drove all the way up to Tillytown right after school, only to find that the farmer had misunderstood her, thinking she wanted African blue basil, not blue-tip basil. Almost in tears, Meredith asked him if he had any idea where she could find what she was looking for. He looked at her like she had two heads and asked her what on Earth was blue-tip basil.

Meredith was in despair. She drove back to Lovelace completely dejected, not knowing what to do next. She spent hours thinking about it and came to only one conclusion. She would have to find a reasonable substitute and pray that Tess couldn't tell the difference.

When she arrived home, she went right to her computer and researched different kinds of basil. Based on what she read, she determined that her best option was sweet basil. She also would add a drop of anise extract, for some said blue-tip basil had the faint essence of licorice. She didn't know if it would work, but she had no choice, and she set about procuring sweet basil and anise extract, and hiding them at the bottom of her bag.

Friday afternoon she stopped home for just a few minutes to change clothes and grab her bags before heading out to Frederick, where Shane would meet her at his parents' house. On her way back out to the car she encountered Wes, who was sitting on his front porch with a newspaper and a beer. She waved in a friendly manner as if nothing awkward had ever happened, and watched as he hesitantly waved back. She sensed him watching her as she threw her bags into the backseat of her car and climbed into the driver's seat, wondering what he was thinking she was doing leaving her house Friday night with an overnight bag, and shuddering.

She pulled out of her driveway without looking at him again, then drove to Frederick with her heart in her throat, feeling that this was it, her one and only chance to make it right with the Thayers. For some reason she believed that if she couldn't do it now, she never would.

～

THE SENATOR MEREDITH knew was staying in his townhouse in Washington that night, having had a late appointment. He would arrive home the following afternoon, after Tess and Maribel helped Meredith choose a wedding gown. After lunch, they would speak with the florist and caterer, then join Shane, Roger, Peter, and the senator for dinner that evening. The following day, Sunday, they would spend at the Thayers' home, and Meredith would prepare Tess's birthday dinner for the entire family.

Meredith hit heavy construction halfway to Frederick and arrived at the Thayers' house very late, well after dinner and shortly after Tess had gone to bed. She was unhappy to have been late, fearing that this would be yet another strike against her, but she was pleased that she wouldn't have to deal with Tess until the following day. She called Shane to let him know she would be late, and he told her to text him when she arrived so he could meet her outside. As she pulled off the road in front of the Thayers' house, she sent Shane a quick text. Moments later, the door opened, and he emerged, looking strong and muscular in tan shorts and a red t-shirt. Meredith watched him as he strode toward her car. The circumstances of this wedding certainly were not ideal, and she had her doubts about whether they made a suitable match, but she had to admit that as time had passed she had grown more and more attracted to him. She didn't know if that attraction further justified her marrying him or was obscuring from her the fact that she shouldn't be.

"Hey," he said as she stepped out of the car. He reached into the backseat and grabbed her bags, then waited for her on the sidewalk. When she was standing next to him, she lifted her face toward his and met him in a kiss that lasted longer than she had thought it would.

"Mmm, you're such a tease," he said with a grin when they pulled away from each other. "The wedding's only a few weeks away. Are you sure you want a separate room? I mean, we're practically married."

"There's still time for you to back out," she said, smiling.

"I'm sure if you let me stay with you tonight, I'd have no desire to back out."

"Just the same, I think I'll stick to my original plan."

"You're the boss."

They walked into the house and tiptoed up the stairs, where Shane showed her to her room. He turned on the light and shut the door, then stood with his hands in his pockets, looking around.

Meredith glanced about the room. It was decorated with tasteful rose patterns and delicate white linens. She felt more at ease in this room than she had in the rest of the house, with its large, imposing furniture and dark colors.

"It's pretty," she said.

He was staring at her, and she stood there awkwardly. She didn't know what to do now.

He stepped toward her, then kissed her forehead and squeezed her shoulder. "All right, I'm out." He headed for the door. "Oh," he said as he opened it, standing halfway in and halfway out. "Mom wanted me to tell you to be downstairs and ready to go at eight-thirty tomorrow morning. Don't be late."

"Okay," she said. "Thanks."

"'Night," he said, smiling, and kissed the air. He closed the door and walked away.

Meredith stared after him, surprised by how disappointed she felt that he had left, and how lonely. Sighing, she changed into her pajamas and washed up in the bathroom that adjoined her room. Then she climbed into bed, feeling restless and thoughtful.

After about ten minutes of tossing and turning, she realized she was very hungry. She hadn't eaten any dinner, but in her despair over being so late and her worry about the weekend, she had forgotten. She felt weak and uncomfortable, and she knew she'd never be able to sleep unless she ate something first. Reluctantly she rose from bed and slipped into her bathrobe and slippers, then slowly, silently exited her room and tiptoed down the stairs, terrified of being caught but feeling famished enough to risk it.

"Oh," she exclaimed with a start as she entered the kitchen. To her great surprise, Shane was sitting at the kitchen table, scrolling through his phone by the light of a small chandelier above. He had a bag of pretzels open next to him on the table and a glass of water next to that.

He turned when she spoke and raised his eyebrows with surprise. "Hey," he said, looking her over. "Nice pajamas." He turned back to his phone and slid his hand inside the bag of pretzels.

She decided food could wait; it seemed a good time to try to engage him in conversation about the weekend. Ignoring the nagging emptiness in her stomach, she walked toward the table and sat down across from him, crossing her legs and folding her hands on her lap. Without looking up, he pushed the opening of the bag toward her and crunched a pretzel loudly.

She stuck her hand inside the bag and withdrew a pretzel, and munched it hungrily. When she quickly took another, he looked up at her.

"Do you want some dinner?"

"Yes, please," she said, unable to resist. "That would be great."

He went to the refrigerator and removed several containers of leftovers, which he placed on a plate and heated in the microwave. As he waited, he leaned against the countertop and crossed his arms. He stared at the floor for a minute in silence, then shifted his gaze to her as she sat at the table.

His face turned into a pleasant smile. "All set for tomorrow?"

"I think so," she responded, turning her legs and body toward him and returning his smile. "It will be good practice for the future."

"What do you mean?"

"I'm assuming I'm going to be spending a lot more time with your mother once you and I get married."

He said nothing. The food finished heating, and he removed it, grabbed a fork from a drawer, and placed the plate in front of her. As she began eating, he poured her a glass of water and placed that beside her plate.

"Thank you," she said gratefully. "This is delicious. Did you make it?"

"No, my mom did."

Meredith ate heartily. He took his seat across from her and flipped through a magazine that was lying on the table.

She swallowed and looked at him. "So I guess this is what it will be like, eating leftovers together in the middle of the night."

He nodded, deep in thought, but said nothing.

She searched for something to say.

"Why don't you ever play the piano? You play so beautifully."

He looked up at her briefly, then back down at the magazine.

"I don't know. I don't like to play for people."

"But you played for all those people at the restaurant."

He took a deep breath; his face grew a little cross. "I was performing then. I don't perform for people I know."

Meredith wasn't sure if he meant he didn't play for people he knew or that he didn't put on an act for people he knew. She sat with his answer for a minute, trying to parse it out.

She had one more question, and she asked it despite knowing she probably shouldn't.

"Would you ever play for me?"

"Like I said," he answered, shoving a pretzel into his mouth and turning the page of the magazine. "I don't like to." He glanced up at her, appearing to try to lessen the effect of his words. "Nothing personal."

She seemed to have irritated him, as she'd suspected she would. In the back of her mind, it occurred to her that his refusal to play for her, his future wife, somehow meant more than it appeared, that it foreshadowed disconnect in their future. But that was silly. It was just a piano; he'd probably been forced to play it his entire life. It was probably one more thing Tess had pushed him into. She decided to let it go. She finished her dinner in silence.

Finally she stood and brought her plate to the sink, where she washed it, dried it, and put it away. He rose and met her at the sink and was in front of her when she turned.

He was close enough for her to touch him, which she did; she wrapped her arms around his waist and leaned in to meet his kiss. He squeezed her hips, and she didn't object when his fingers slinked under her shirt and brushed the skin of her waist and back. Encouraged by the fact that she had not protested, he let his hands roam from her waist to her breasts, where his fingers gripped and explored her hurriedly, expecting her to stop him at any time.

She couldn't help but admire his solid strength as he pressed himself to her, the way his clothes strained against the almost immodest thickness of him. Without thinking, she lifted her knee to move her leg around him. A long sigh escaped her throat.

He seemed to sense her faltering, and he whispered in her ear. "Come on, babe. What are we waiting for?"

"There's so little time before the wedding," she breathed. "Let's wait."

He groaned in an exaggerated manner and pretended to bite her throat, tickling her. She laughed.

"You're killing me here," he said, grabbing her shoulders and pulling away. "Are you sure you want to wait?" He raised his eyebrows and put his hands in the air. "I've been told I'm pretty good."

She giggled and blushed. "I'm sure you are. But I promised myself."

He took a deep breath and smiled. "Okay," he said. "But I might explode before then. I'm just warning you."

"If you do, you can blame me."

"It's a deal."

WHEN MEREDITH RETURNED to her room, she saw that she had just missed a call from Tara. Surprised, she climbed into bed and called her back.

"What are you doing up so late?" Meredith asked when her friend picked up.

"Tom and the girls are at his mother's," Tara told her. "I'm going to stay up all night and enjoy the silence. How's your weekend going? Has Tess bitten your head off yet?"

"No," Meredith said, settling in and running her fingers through her hair. "I arrived too late. Tess was already in bed."

"Lucky you. Squeeze in as much Tess-free time as you can before you're required to see her."

They said nothing for several moments.

"So how's Shane?"

"He's good," Meredith replied, ignoring the forced enthusiasm she sensed in Tara's voice. "You know, I'm really starting to like him."

"That's just because you've accepted a new normal. You've now become used to people treating you like crap, and it looks good to you."

Meredith frowned. "That's not true. He's just different. He has a lot going on. He means well, but he's learning how to be in a serious relationship."

"You're making excuses for him."

"No, I'm not," Meredith said, a bit testily now. "Nobody's perfect, Tara. I can accept Shane for who he is."

"But why? You're so quick to defend Shane. Why defend him and no one else?"

"What's that supposed to mean?"

"It means that you need your other relationships to be perfect, but somehow with Shane you're willing to accept anything. As hard a time as you had with Wes, he was a hundred times better for you than Shane. And yet you staunchly insist he'll never change. Then there's Nick. I think you should call him back and tell him you didn't mean what you said, that you don't want to marry Shane after all."

"What would be the point? Nick told me to marry Shane. He said he wanted me to do it."

"He lied to you, Merry. He told you to marry Shane because he thought you wanted to marry him, because that's what you told him."

"You have no idea how badly I want that to be true," Meredith said with tears in her voice. "But if it were, he'd be brave enough to come back. He would do it regardless of anything else. He wouldn't push me away."

"You mean like you're pushing him away right now?"

"Are you trying to say it's my fault?"

"Of course not. But honestly, Merry, I think you made a mistake. You should have told him the truth instead of testing him like you did. You put him in an impossible situation. What was he supposed to say?"

Meredith couldn't keep the anger out of her voice. "Why did you call me, Tara? I'm getting married in three weeks. I don't need this."

"I'm sorry. Don't be mad." Tara took a breath while she gathered her thoughts, and then spoke again, more calmly. "I just want to see you happy. That's all. It makes me sad to see you so afraid. I hate that you're settling because you don't want to be alone. Maybe some time alone would even be good for you."

"Just forget it. You just can't understand."

"Then explain it to me, Merry," Tara pleaded. "Please, make me understand."

A tense pause followed as Meredith decided how to respond.

"It isn't that I don't want to be alone," she said finally. "I've been alone before, and I can do it again. But I can't stand the uncertainty." Tears pricked in her eyes: it wasn't just the break-ups. She had been suddenly hit with a memory, not of an event but of a feeling—a feeling of being in suspense, of knowing Adam was dying but of not knowing when, or how—of being aware that the process of his being pulled away from her would begin at any moment. She swallowed hard; these were difficult things to say. "It needs to be over," she told Tara, simply. "The instability. I need to pick a path so I can be sure what's going to happen."

"That's not a good enough reason."

"You can't say that unless you've been in my shoes."

Another few moments of silence passed.

Meredith said, "In any case, I don't need it to be perfect. Nick and Wes thought it had to be perfect. That's why it didn't work out with them."

"That has nothing to do with right now. You've convinced yourself you're playing it safe, but I'm worried that you're playing with fire."

"I know what I'm doing. Don't worry about me."

"That's easy for you to say. You don't love you like I do."

"But I do, Tara. And that's why I'm doing this. It's simple with Shane. He doesn't care if it's perfect. He's actually the safest of them all."

MEREDITH WAS tired and had little trouble falling asleep that night. She slept fitfully, however, and woke up when the sun was barely peeking up over the horizon, not yet reaching her window. Bleary-eyed, she rose and dressed, choosing a light blue sundress and white sweater, and blowing out her hair so that it fell straight and soft to her shoulders. She cleaned up her room, making her bed tidily, and crept downstairs with a book in hand, not knowing who was awake. She had the intention of eating a light breakfast at the kitchen table with the comfort of her book, hoping to settle her nerves. Any minute now she would encounter Tess.

She was just walking toward the kitchen when she heard the front door open. When she turned, Shane was standing in the doorway, his head lowered so he could watch his feet, as if his looking at them could make them more quiet. He tiptoed inside and shut the door as gently as he could, then turned around and nearly jumped out of his shoes when he saw her standing before him.

"Hi," she said. "What are you doing?"

"Hey, babe." He smiled as he approached, then kissed her. "I just had to run out to my car for a second. I can't find the piece of paper where I wrote down the name of the flower I was thinking of for the wedding. I saw this flower the other day and thought it would look good in the centerpieces."

"Oh," she said, surprised, her eyes wide. "That's nice. What did the flower look like?"

"I can't describe it. It was white, and it had a lot of petals."

"See if you can find that paper," Meredith responded with a giggle. "Hey, why are you still wearing your clothes from yesterday?"

"Oh, yeah," he said, looking down at himself. "Last night after you went upstairs I watched a little TV on the couch, but I fell asleep." He rubbed her shoulders, a crooked grin on his face. "You really had me going last night. I couldn't sleep worth a damn."

"Sorry," she said, with a grin of her own. "I guess I shouldn't kiss you anymore before the wedding, either."

"It's okay. I like when you get me going."

They were interrupted by the sound of footsteps on the stairs. Tess was descending the staircase, wearing navy dress slacks and a matching jacket, a white blouse peeking from underneath. Meredith felt her heartbeat quicken but put on her most charming smile and straightened as she prepared to greet her future mother-in-law.

Just then Maribel, in a crimson wraparound dress, strode in through the front door, without knocking, and noticed them standing in the foyer. Her face brightened, and she hurried inside to embrace them both. Tess, her face darker, followed more slowly and brought each in for a lukewarm hug, then spoke to Shane as Maribel engaged Meredith in light conversation about her evening.

Maribel drew Meredith by the arm into the kitchen while Tess stayed behind with Shane. Once out of earshot, Maribel turned to Meredith and whispered in her ear.

"I'm going to make this day as pleasant as possible. Okay?"

"Thank you," Meredith whispered in return, utterly grateful. "You're a good friend."

"You mean sister," Maribel said, and squeezed Meredith's hand.

The two women returned to the foyer, where Maribel suggested they go out for breakfast before their appointment at the bridal salon. Shane kissed Meredith goodbye; then the three women piled into Maribel's car and headed to a nearby café for breakfast.

Tess was chilly but receptive to conversation and did not shirk from answering Meredith's polite attempts at small talk. She managed to ask Meredith a few questions about her life and interests, clearly doing so out of obligation but meeting that obligation nonetheless. She was cordial even when, in response to Maribel's referring to her as "the future Mrs. Thayer," Meredith nervously clarified that she was keeping her name; Meredith wasn't sure whether Tess's nonchalance on this subject meant she was trying to be conciliatory or that she was secretly pleased Meredith wouldn't officially be a Thayer, but the discussion was polite, and that was all Meredith cared about. Maribel continued to gracefully draw them into common conversations, and as Meredith had not been insulted or challenged, by the end of the hour she considered the breakfast a success.

When they arrived at the salon, they were shown to a spacious, almost unbearably ornate room with lush white couches and striped wallpaper. Meredith slipped into dozens of dresses, each time gazing with amazement at herself in the mirror as she stepped onto a stool and imagined herself as a bride. Tess and Maribel offered their opinions, Maribel clapping her hands together with delight or scrunching her face with disapproval as she stood with Meredith in the mirror, Tess remaining seated, relaying her opinions by the degree of sneer she wore on her face.

Finally Meredith found her dress, and even Tess was inspired to stand and admire as Meredith stood staring at the vision in the mirror, enraptured by the image, not believing she could be looking at herself. The dress was a clean strapless satin A-line, with delicate Chantilly lace adorning her on either side in wide, straight panels from the bodice down to the long chapel train. It was simple but elegant, and the three women stood back and took deep breaths.

"Oh, Meredith," cooed Maribel, with tears in her eyes. "You look stunning."

"Thank you," Meredith said quietly, unable to take her eyes off the image in the mirror.

"Mom, isn't it perfect? Doesn't she look beautiful?"

"Yes," Tess replied. "She does."

Meredith turned to Tess. For once Tess met her gaze, and if Meredith hadn't known better she would have thought she saw something like softness there. She took this as approval, and on a whim she placed her hand on Tess's shoulder and kissed her cheek. Tess said nothing, but as Meredith returned her attention to the mirror she saw the shadow of a smile touch Tess's eyes.

Meredith took one last look at herself before changing back into her own clothes. This was it; it was really happening. She was finally achieving the stability and security she thought she wanted. She stepped off the stool she was standing on, but she wavered and nearly toppled over. Maribel caught her and asked her if she was okay. Meredith smiled and assured her she was. She stumbled to the dressing room and took off the gown, replacing it with her blue sundress and white sweater. She looked at herself in the mirror; her face was as white as her dress. For a second she imagined what it would feel like to open the door of the dressing room and find not Tess and Maribel standing there, but Sarah and Helen—but she quickly put that thought out of her mind and joined the women who would be her family for the rest of her life.

Tess, Maribel, and Meredith returned to the Thayers' home to eat a quick lunch before driving over to the country club to speak with the caterer and florist. Meredith noticed a new car in the driveway and assumed it was the senator's; her heart began racing with anxiety, but she needn't have worried, as he did not emerge from his office while they were there. The three women sat at the dining room table eating sandwiches and chatting awkwardly about their morning. Shane soon joined them and took a seat across from Meredith.

"Shane, I can't wait to see the look on your face when you see Meredith in that dress," Maribel gushed. "She is going to be a sight, for sure. You'll die."

Shane smiled and turned to Meredith. "I'm sure she will be."

"I'm so happy for you two," Maribel continued. "Mom, I'll bet you never guessed Shane would settle down with someone as nice as Meredith."

"No, I never did," said Tess, and Meredith avoided looking at her, not wanting to know if she was being ironic.

"So what's next on the agenda?" Shane asked, leaning on the table, his hands folded together.

"We see the caterer and the florist," said Maribel. "Then we'll come home, and we can all go out to dinner. Won't that be fun?"

"Shane," said Meredith suddenly, turning to him, "did you ever remember the name of that flower?"

Maribel and Tess looked at Meredith with blank stares.

"Flower?" inquired Tess.

"Shane told me this morning that he saw a flower he wanted in the wedding," Meredith informed them, smiling brightly. "He had written it on a piece of paper, but he couldn't find it."

Maribel and Tess then looked at Shane, their faces incredulous.

Shane straightened and placed his hands on the table face down. "What?" he said defensively, turning his hands on their sides. "Can't I like a flower?"

Maribel furrowed her brow and smirked. "I guess so," she said. "So what was it? What was the flower?"

"Meredith just told you—I can't remember. Damn, why doesn't everyone stop giving me the third degree?"

Everyone stared at him. He looked around the table with wide eyes, then smiled. "Sorry," he said, scratching his head. "I guess I'm a little tense. I can't remember the name of that bloody flower. Just pick whatever you want; I'm sure I'll love it." He stood then and walked to the other side of the table to kiss Meredith briskly before he strode out of the room, telling them to have a good time and that he'd see them all later.

Meredith turned back to Maribel and Tess, who were looking at each other with expressions Meredith couldn't read. After a few awkward moments they both resumed their breathing and fiddled with their plates.

"All right, then," Maribel said with a smile as she stood. "Shall we?"

~

THE REMAINDER of the afternoon was uncomfortable for Meredith as she, Tess, and Maribel spoke at length with vendors at the site of the wedding. It wasn't long before she understood that most decisions were best left to Tess and Maribel, who were more knowledgeable and who seemed to care much more than she did about the details that would occupy mere hours of Meredith's life. She was indifferent about these details; she was more concerned with what would follow, what she would face the day after.

At dinner that night, the Thayers chatted amongst themselves about everything except the wedding. Meredith had been looking forward to trying to bond with them but soon realized that there were more important events than her marriage to Shane, and she sat back to listen and try to lose herself in her own thoughts. Senator Thayer attempted a few jokes at her father's expense; Meredith did not take the bait, responding with vague, polite answers and consoling herself that after the wedding she and Shane wouldn't have to see them if they didn't want to.

Meredith eventually welcomed their talking around her; it gave her the chance to retreat into her own mind. Tomorrow she was cooking Tess's birthday dinner. She would need all the mental preparation she could get.

WHEN THEY ARRIVED BACK at the house, they all said a brisk goodnight and went to their rooms. Meredith was just coming out of her bathroom when she heard the doorknob turn, and then Shane was in her room, shutting the door quietly as he entered.

"Hey," he whispered, going to her with a sly grin on his face. "This is kind of fun. I feel like I'm in high school again."

"You mean sneaking around, trying not to get caught by the parents? No thanks. I'll take adulthood any day."

"The one difference is that they can't do anything to us now," he said, wrapping his arms around her and pushing her toward the bed.

She let him fall on top of her, amazed by how heavy he felt and by the bulkiness of his shoulders, chest, and back under her hands. He was trying to persuade her by acting as if this were the kind of thing they did all the time, by reminding her of what she was missing. Remembering the latitude she had given him the night before, he slid his hand down the back of her dress and, with shocking quickness and skill, unclasped her bra from behind.

"What are you doing?" she gasped as he shifted on top of her.

"What does it look like I'm doing? I'm trying to get you into bed."

"I told you that—"

"I know what you told me. I think I can change your mind."

She mindlessly placed her hand on his back as he nuzzled his face into her neck, kissing her shoulder and sliding his lips toward her chest.

"Shane," she said, her chin lifted toward the ceiling. "Shane, please."

"Please what?" he asked, and looked at her.

She didn't know. She had been protesting out of habit, but she didn't really want him to stop.

"I don't think this is a good idea," she said.

"I'll tell you what," he responded, his voice taking on a tone of calm practicality. "We just keep going like this until you're ready to stop, and then we'll stop. Just say the word. How does that sound?"

She suppressed a grin. She wasn't sure if he was trying to be funny, but he was on the verge of making her laugh. She wanted to keep going. She figured, *What the hell?*

"Okay."

"Great," he said, and stuck his hand up her dress.

At first he amused her by working so hard, trying to prove that he was capable of turning her around; he was so serious as to be almost comical, and she praised him to indulge his ego, not wanting to hurt his feelings. But as he continued, removing his shirt and deepening his kiss, holding her thigh in his hand and grabbing her seductively from behind, she began to worry, and opened her eyes.

"Shane, I think you'd better stop now," she said, making her voice firm.

"If you're telling me to stop, it only means you want me to keep going."

"It doesn't matter. I'm telling you to stop."

"Let me keep going. You won't be sorry."

She didn't say anything more, but closed her eyes again and tried to hide the fact that her breaths had grown heavy. She was trying to think, but her mind was becoming foggy. Her heart began beating in a quick pattern, a pattern she hadn't heard in months; she felt a familiar tingle in her blood, and she sighed, melting into him.

He sensed her relax and took advantage of her weakening. A hoarse groan escaping him, he pulled her dress up over her hips and backside, his lips still on hers.

"Shane," she whispered, to stop him, but she was allowing him to spread her knees, already imagining the feel of him inside her, and liking it.

He ignored her, both hands now caressing her thighs, rubbing them up and down and moving to her waist, getting ready to undress her completely. He slipped his fingers between her legs and probed her, tentatively enough to wait for her reaction but confidently enough to suggest that he didn't think she would stop him.

She arched her back and exhaled sharply, memories of joyful possibilities flooding back to her as his fingers both satisfied her and set her further on fire. They circled and pressed, and as she drifted further toward giving in he made his caresses more tender, more intimate, in the hopes of weakening her defenses. She opened her legs wide for his thick forearm, and he dug into her forcefully, pleased to have made it this far.

She opened her eyes again. "Shane, you need to stop now."

"Come on, babe," he whispered silkily. "Aren't you having a good time?"

"Yes," she gasped.

He dug deeper and kissed her behind her ear.

"Shane, stop," she insisted, and tried to sit up, believing it was as far as she could go and still turn back. "Stop!"

At last he stopped and withdrew his arm. "Christ, Meredith," he hissed as he sat up and prepared to leave. "You have the patience of a saint, and not in a good way."

"We've been over this. I told you I wanted to wait."

"Nobody asked me how I felt about that. Christ!" he exclaimed, and shook his head, frustrated.

Meredith didn't know what to say. She was sorry for upsetting him but not sorry for keeping her promise to herself. She hoped he would tell her he understood, that he could wait another few weeks, that she was worth it.

He stood and straightened his clothing. "For all your talk about being an adult, you sure hold out like a scared teenager." He looked at her. "How old are you, anyway?"

Meredith stared at him, thinking quickly of when she must have told him her age and realizing with shock that it had never come up.

"I'm thirty-four."

"That's too old to wait this long." He turned to leave. "Thanks for nothing." He walked out and closed the door.

Meredith lay on the bed staring up at the ceiling. She wished Shane at least had turned off the light before stalking out. She stood up, shut off the light, and climbed back into bed in her dress. Then she lay there deliberately pretending the last ten minutes had not happened. Instead she imagined herself lying next to Nick, tried to remember how it had felt to fall asleep to his gentle kisses. When she remembered that he had rejected her yet again, giving her up, she frowned and put him out of her mind. Instead she thought about Wes, how he used to slide his leg between hers, teasing and inviting her. But thoughts of Wes turned to his insistent demands, and she pushed him aside as well. She lay there alone, stewing angrily, until she finally fell asleep, wondering why it was that she continued to put herself through this.

CHAPTER NINE

THE FUTURE

*M*eredith awoke the next morning exhausted, her first thought of how Shane had embarrassed her the previous night, her second thought of how today was the day she was to prepare Tess's birthday dinner. She felt an overwhelming sense of doom as she showered and dressed, but she tried to put her worries out of her mind. She stared at herself in the mirror for a moment or two before taking a deep breath, opening the door, and descending the staircase for breakfast.

Shane was sitting on a chair in the foyer by the foot of the stairs. He looked up and promptly stood as she approached.

"Hey," he said, placing his hands on her shoulders. "I was a total asshole last night. I'm sorry."

"It's okay," she said, too nervous to be concerned about it at the moment. "I'm over it."

"Listen, I don't mind waiting," he said, and smiled. "Not that I wouldn't be thrilled if you changed your mind."

"Thanks, Shane. I appreciate that."

He was frowning. "Seriously, Meredith. I hope I didn't hurt your feelings. You don't deserve to be yelled at."

Meredith's eyes softened with gratitude. "Thanks," she said again, flustered and overcome. "That's nice of you."

He patted her shoulders, his expression turning more upbeat. "Are we good?"

"Yes," she said, nervous again, "just as long as I can pull off this dinner."

"Don't worry about it. You know how to cook. It'll be fine."

"I hope so," she said absentmindedly, thinking of her basil.

Meredith received little attention from Shane's family and took to the kitchen shortly before lunch, ready to begin preparations for dinner. Everyone left her alone in the kitchen, with the exception of Suzanne, the housekeeper, who came in from time to time to perform various tasks and to help Meredith, who didn't want or need the help. She didn't even want to be distracted by Shane, who joined her occasionally to check in. She smiled up at him and returned his kisses, patting his arm and telling him she was fine, to go enjoy the time he had with his family. When the time came for her to make her sneaky substitution, she peered with caution around the corner to make sure she wasn't being watched; she hastily chopped her sweet basil and added a small drop of anise extract, then stole upstairs to return them to her room. When the dishes were ready to cook, she was able to relax a bit, and she went back to her room to change and regroup before the final sprint toward dinner.

Meredith was serving not just the family but also Caroline and Victoria, Roger's girlfriend. Meredith gathered from the boisterous conversation she heard coming from the foyer as Victoria arrived that Tess approved of her, and she sneered in her head, wondering what it took to get on Tess's good side.

When Caroline arrived, Meredith tried to pay special attention to the activity in the foyer outside the kitchen, but the noise level had increased since everyone had changed for dinner, and she could hear little of the conversation. When they began whispering, Meredith's ears perked up, but she was unable to detect what was being said. She concentrated on her work, determined to impress them that night.

Finally it was time. Meredith wiped her brow and looked around, proud and relieved. Everything had come out just right. As Shane entered the room and scanned the dishes, he nodded, impressed.

"Wow."

Meredith was pleased, and she smiled in spite of her nervousness. He wrapped his arm around her back and pulled her close, congratulating her.

"It looks like you pulled it off," he said. "Nice work."

"It remains to be seen," she noted, nodding as her eyes surveyed her accomplishments, "but I think it will be okay."

"It's nice of you to do this for my mother. Maybe nicer than she deserves. I hope she appreciates it."

"Honestly, Shane, I didn't just do this for your mother," she told him, looking up into his face. "I did this for myself."

They drew everyone into the dining room and sat down, ready for Suzanne to help bring in the dishes and serve. Meredith's heart was beating so hard she wasn't sure she'd be able to sit still, and when Maribel began a polite conversation with her she was so breathy and distracted she had to deliberately focus on Maribel's face, trying her best to act naturally but sure her anxiety was obvious.

Senator Thayer took his seat at the head of the table and sat straight, his attention turned to Meredith and his face wearing a wide grin. "Let's see how you did, Miss Beck," he barked as he placed his napkin on his lap. "Maybe it will be enough to satisfy Tess, in which case you can call your father and tell him the wedding is still on. As awkward as it'll be having him as an in-law, part of me relishes the chance to make him uncomfortable." He laughed in a dramatic fashion. "Tess, are you ready?" he asked, turning to his wife and pretending to scratch the air with his fingers. "Put your claws on!"

As Senator Thayer moved on, turning his attention to Roger, Meredith did not respond. She tried to relax her shoulders and to wear a confident smile. As dinner was served, she sneaked a glance around the table, taking note of the reactions. So far no one had grimaced or spat anything out. Maribel complimented her profusely, much to the annoyance of Caroline, who said nothing but whose stony face spoke more than any words.

"Caroline," said Tess as her fork pressed into a crab cake, and Meredith was sure she would faint to the floor, "I hear your sister will be getting engaged soon. How lovely! Please congratulate her for me. We're all very excited for her."

"Thank you so much, Tess. I'm sure your good wishes will mean a lot to her."

Meredith hid a frown but couldn't help staring at Tess with disbelief, wondering how she could be so hurtful. Here Meredith had gone out of her way to prepare a complicated meal for Tess's birthday, had asked to do it and had worked all day, had prepared in advance, to make sure it was perfect—the least Tess could do was thank her, or not talk about someone else's wedding as if it were more important than hers. She was growing tired of working so hard to please a woman who seemed intent on not being pleased, who would sooner minimize the importance of her own son's wedding than be nice to Meredith, just because of some silly article written by her father years before. She knew Tess preferred Caroline, but she and Tess had had so little time to get to know each other. If Tess would only open her heart to her, she might find that she, too, was good enough for her son.

During the time she had been thinking, Meredith's eyes had fallen to the table. Sharply she returned her gaze to Tess to discern her reaction to the crab cake. Tess was staring at her plate, her face still, having paused mid-chew; Meredith could see that she was holding the bite in her mouth. When Tess swallowed, slowly, her face contorted into an expression of wicked pleasure, and at that moment Meredith knew there was nothing she could ever do to please her, that Tess would be only too grateful to find fault with Meredith and that she was looking forward to doing what she was about to do.

"Interesting," Tess said, delicately replacing her fork on her plate and resting her forearm on the table. She turned to Shane. "Shane, dear—have you tried the crab cakes?"

"Not yet."

"Hmm," she said, and took a sip of water.

Caroline's eyes widened, and she eagerly tasted a small bite of crab cake; however, it was clear from her face that she couldn't determine the problem. She looked at Meredith, disappointed not to be in on the secret.

"What's wrong with the crab cakes?" asked Senator Thayer. He took a big bite and shrugged.

"Shane, I'd be curious to hear your thoughts," Tess said. "There's something about it; I just can't place it. Ah," she said then, holding her finger in the air, and judging from the contrived manner with which she spoke Meredith was sure Tess had all along known what had happened. "Meredith, were you able to find the blue-tip basil?" she asked, though Meredith knew Tess already knew the answer to that question, and resented being baited. Tess grinned. "I think I know what you were trying to do," she said. "Sweet basil isn't a bad substitution, dear, but it's a bit too mild to pass as blue-tip basil. How did you manage the licorice essence? Anise extract?"

"Yes, that's right," she said, caring less and less about Tess and her opinions with each passing moment. "I was unable to find the blue-tip basil. I drove two hours after work on Thursday to a farm in Tillytown, only to find that the farmer had misunderstood me and had the wrong basil. By then it was too late. I thought I could make an appropriate substitution and that no one would be the worse for it."

"It was foolish of you," said Tess. "Had you been upfront, we of course would have understood your predicament. I'm disappointed that you thought so little of us as to think we would hold it against you. As it is, your attempt to hoodwink us is, I have to say, a little insulting. I don't appreciate being tricked, especially on my birthday."

"Christ, Mom," Shane said. "Chill out. It's just some freaking basil."

"That's not the point, dear."

Senator Thayer laughed. "I was going to miss dinner tonight to attend a party at Vern's, but I'm glad I stayed," he said, and clapped. "This is much more entertaining."

"Excuse me," Meredith interjected. "I have something to say."

Everyone stared at her. Meredith looked around the table. All eyes were on her, save for Senator Thayer's; he was tucking into his dinner as if nothing were happening.

Meredith turned to Tess. "It's true that I made the substitution without drawing attention to it. It's only because I wanted to impress you, because I wanted to do something nice for you on your birthday. I should have been upfront with you, but I was worried that it would overshadow the fact that my heart was in the right place." She paused here, hoping her meaning was getting through. "My only desire was to please you and to show you that I'm eager to be part of your family. I hope you can forgive my indiscretion and accept me as one of you. I think that's what this day should be about—love and tolerance—and not about a silly mistake that was made with nothing but good intentions." She paused again and swallowed, her heart beating so quickly she thought it would take flight in her chest. "I made this dinner as a gift to you, to try to make you happy, and I hope you will accept it, knowing that I had you in mind as I prepared it."

Nobody spoke. Tess was staring at her, her eyebrows furrowed crossly as she considered what Meredith had said.

The silence was interrupted by Caroline.

"That's not true," she said. Her back straight, her hands folded in her lap, she faced Tess. "Tess, I heard Meredith telling Shane that she didn't do this for you, that she did this for herself." She turned to Meredith. "Isn't that right, Meredith? Didn't you say that to Shane?"

Meredith felt long fingers of heat creep from her chest and over her neck, chin, cheeks, and ears until her entire face was burning. Her eyes focused sharply on Caroline, she made herself speak.

"Yes, Caroline, I said that. You must have exceptional hearing."

Caroline's eyes narrowed, and her cheeks lost a bit of color, but Meredith didn't notice; she was pushing her chair back and standing. Without a word she turned and walked from the room, tossing her napkin onto the kitchen counter as she stalked through. She went upstairs to her room, where she began packing her bag to go home.

She had a sudden urge to call Wes, to be comforted by the sound of his voice and to hear him call her "sweetheart" with that charming lilt in his voice. She wanted to listen to his logic, to hear him laugh with her and try to impress her, to let him be her friend. Somehow at that moment Wes was the only person she wanted to talk to but the one person she knew to whom she couldn't turn.

She began throwing things into her suitcase, but she didn't have much time to reflect on what had happened before her door opened, and Shane walked in. Meredith looked to see who it was but turned her face away as he approached.

"They slaughtered me down there, and you did nothing to stop it."

"Come on, babe. Do you really think I could have stopped it?"

"You could have at least tried."

"I've been trying for thirty years. Trust me, there's nothing I could have done."

"Shane, I just don't think I can do this."

Neither of them spoke for several agonizing moments.

Suddenly his hands were on her shoulders. He turned her around to face him.

"Why don't you stay," he said, and patted her arms. "Don't worry about them. Let's just do our thing and let them self-destruct."

Meredith frowned. "I don't know, Shane. As much as you say that, you're still a part of them."

"But I don't want to be. I want you to stay. Look, I'm trying here. Isn't that a good enough reason for you to try too?"

The door opened again. In stepped Maribel, who went to Meredith and took her hand.

"Meredith, I'm so sorry. I don't know what got into Caroline. And Mom's just Mom."

"What should I do, Maribel? Will it ever get better? Is it worth it?"

"That's up to you," said Maribel, her eyes wide and soft. "I hope you decide that it is. I'm sure Mom will warm over time. And as for Caroline, she's just jealous. But you're the one marrying Shane."

Meredith sighed. "I need to think. It's just too bad I can't predict the future."

"The future is in your hands," replied Maribel. "You just have to decide what you want it to be."

MEREDITH MADE the drive home in silence, no music or phone. She had to decide what she wanted for the rest of her life. It seemed a big decision to make in an hour, but that is what her life had come to. She felt that her ability to make serious decisions was being stretched to the limit. Too frequently in the last year she had been forced to think about the path of her life, had been required to alter that path or stay on it, depending on events far into the future that she could not predict. She was weary and numb. She couldn't do it anymore.

For mostly this reason she decided to go through with her wedding. She was beyond tired. She had suffered so much emotional turmoil that she wasn't thinking clearly, and knew she wasn't. She knew this was a reason not to marry Shane. But she also knew that marrying him would eliminate the necessity of making any future decisions. She needed to rest. If that rest had to be with the Thayers, so be it.

Also she was curious to see where her relationship with Shane would lead. He was unpredictable and moody and sometimes childish, but there was something about him that warmed Meredith. He could be sensitive and caring, and his intentions generally seemed to be good. She still wasn't sure why he wanted to marry her—too often he had shown cold indifference toward her—but for some reason he kept begging her to stay. She guessed he had been damaged and that even he wasn't sure why he wanted to be with her. That was acceptable to her. If he wanted her to stay, she could help him be the person he wanted to be. Something in her told her she should try.

But she groaned at the idea of spending her life with the Thayers. She hoped they wouldn't damage her as they had damaged Shane. She hoped Shane was worth becoming one of them.

It was June. Graduation was to take place in two weeks. That weekend would be Meredith's wedding with Shane. Before that happened, Meredith would help the students put on their long-awaited play, grade her term papers, and administer her final exams. It was a busy, tumultuous time, and Meredith was in a constant state of anxiety. She had no way of knowing that it was only the beginning, that her life was about to be consumed by chaos and that she would finally hit rock bottom before she saw the end of the month.

In the midst of her school responsibilities and the stress of planning her wedding, Meredith was plagued constantly by the sight of her neighbors, who had all but abandoned attempts to resume their friendships with her. Ironically the friendliest of all of them was Wes, who at least did not pretend not to have seen her as she drove by, and waved. She had not had much of a chance to speak with him, given all she had to do, but she always knew he was there, watching her from across the street as they went about their lives. This knowledge both unsettled and comforted her; she recoiled from the awkwardness of living across the street from him, but she felt more secure knowing he was so nearby. She knew he would always protect her, no matter what. She sensed that his anger had turned to sadness, that he was grieving but resigned, and she knew that with time he would move on.

He remained cordial and polite with Shane when Shane came to pick her up for a date, even though Shane seemed to go out of his way to flaunt her in front of Wes, a habit Meredith abhorred. She couldn't say anything because she wasn't certain it was deliberate or that she wasn't imagining it. But she continued to pretend it wasn't happening; it was easier that way.

Meredith had never made another attempt to recapture her former closeness with Jodi, and she knew she was partly to blame for their failure to remain friends. She hadn't had the courage or the energy. She had only so much capacity for emotional crises, and somehow her friendship with Jodi did not take priority. She regretted this, but she consoled herself with the knowledge that Jodi had not made any further efforts either.

Meredith was nervous about her house. She didn't see any reason to worry that her wedding would not take place, but soon she would be forced to move regardless, and this fact only added to her stress. She had heard from Tara that Frank and Grace were planning on returning at the end of the summer and that they were interested in selling it to Meredith. However, Meredith was no longer interested in buying it. She and Shane had decided to sell his townhouse and move to the Maryland suburbs of Washington, bringing Shane closer to The Gray Fox and preventing Meredith from having to find a new job. Meredith didn't know how this was supposed to happen in such a short time, but she knew he was receiving help from the Thayers, who put on the appearance of joy in spite of their reservations, and left it at that. At this point she didn't care where she lived. She just wanted it to be over so she could stop thinking.

Oddly the one fact that weighed on her most heavily was that she would no longer have the chance to see Wes every day. She would miss him terribly. Regardless of the strain between them, she still felt a connection with him and hurt deeply at the thought of moving away from him. She felt sad, lonely, and depressed, and she withdrew even further into her own life. Her only comforts were her now frequent conversations with Tara, her dates with Shane, and the companionship of Henry, Katrina, and Scott—though she was getting the feeling they had begun to feel distanced from her as she had drifted further and further down her spiral of anxiety. They tried to retrieve her, but she felt irretrievable, at least until after her wedding, until she had a sense of finality and closure, until a time when she knew she would never again feel the torture of uncertainty.

CHAPTER TEN

PRINCIPLES

One night during the first week of June, Meredith was grading a batch of her seniors' essays when she came across Jason Richter's. As soon as she began reading, she knew she had a problem.

The essay was flawless. It was well argued, well organized, and well executed. It was unlike anything he had written before. Meredith knew with certainty that he had once again attempted to pass off someone else's work as his own.

Frustrated but determined, she opened a new tab and began searching. She isolated key phrases, punching in one after the other until she hit the jackpot. A particular phrase turned up verbatim in her search, and when she clicked on the link she found Jason's entire essay, word for word.

Her heart pounding, she printed the essay and highlighted key words and phrases to make the comparison easier. Part of her was elated, having finally caught Jason in the act of cheating. It would be a good lesson for him. It would redeem her. And it would satisfy her need to right a wrong.

But part of her was terrified. She had no idea how Nancy would receive this. Nancy had told Meredith to return to her when she had evidence of cheating, but she had never said what she would do if and when this was to happen. Meredith would soon find out.

❧

THE NEXT DAY she spoke with Katrina before school and showed her Jason's essay and the essay she had found online. Katrina sneered, saying that Jason had become overly confident from not being caught, making it quite easy for Meredith to catch him this time. She hugged Meredith and told her that her only option was to inform Nancy, and wished her luck, asking that Meredith let her know the result of her conversation.

Meredith went to Nancy without hesitation before she lost her nerve. She explained the situation and showed Nancy the essays.

Nancy looked them over, her face expressionless.

"It's a good thing you discovered this with a couple of weeks left before graduation," said Nancy, returning the papers to Meredith. "Just tell Jason he has two weeks to rewrite the paper, and you'll be fine."

Meredith stared at her in disbelief. "I don't understand. Are you telling me not to penalize him for lifting this paper from the internet?"

"I'm telling you to give him another chance. He has plenty of time to rectify it before he graduates."

Meredith was beyond the point of feeling diplomatic; recent events had made her harder and more stoic, and she almost didn't care what happened anymore. She said, "What you're suggesting is revolting. You're telling me to ignore the fact that he's been cheating all year, disrespecting me and you and himself and all of his classmates. I'm just not sure I can do that."

Nancy looked up from her paperwork and watched Meredith in silence for several moments. Finally, she said, "You don't have a choice. Tell Jason he can rewrite his paper, and don't use the word 'cheat.' That's my answer."

Meredith took the essays in her hand and turned, ready to walk out of the office, dejected and incredulous.

"Meredith," Nancy called her back.

Meredith faced Nancy once more.

"I'll overlook your rudeness this time."

Meredith turned back toward the door and walked out.

FRIDAY NIGHT MEREDITH finished the last of her senior essays. She had submitted all the grades, all except for Jason's. She sat at the kitchen island for many minutes, tapping her pen on the countertop, her face in her hand, her elbow on the table.

She didn't know what to do. It could be her last chance to teach Jason a lesson. To her the answer was obvious. A student had stolen his essay and had to be penalized for it. It wasn't the first time he had done it; he had brazenly been flouting the rules of ethics all year, and at last she had the proof. He couldn't graduate and go into the world thinking this kind of behavior was acceptable. Clearly nobody was going to hold him accountable. What service would she be doing him by following Nancy's orders?

On the other hand, she flinched when she imagined Nancy's reaction once she found out that her wishes had been disregarded. She knew she could very well be fired. The idea of adding this stress to her already overwhelming pile of worries made Meredith sick with anxiety.

But she knew what she had to do. She had had enough. Too many times Jason had tried to pull the wool over her eyes. Too many times he had gotten away with cheating, for no reason other than that his parents were wealthy. Too many times Meredith had been forced to passively watch this behavior go unchecked, and too many times she had regretted not being stronger.

She brought her finger to the zero key and pressed, the round figure stinging her eyes as it filled the space next to the name "Jason Richter." She wrote "See me" in the comments, then sat back to look at it one more time. She closed the tab and shut her laptop. Then she went upstairs to bed.

AFTER MONTHS of planning and countless hours of work, Meredith was delighted to attend the school play. On Saturday, she met Scott and Marianne in the lobby, and the three of them joined Katrina and Craig, as well as Henry and Jay, in the auditorium, their faces bright and eager as they anticipated witnessing the product of their efforts. Meredith looked and felt radiant. It was the culmination of her work that year, in some ways; she was proud of what she had done, of the confidence and skill with which she had armed her students, and she hoped they remembered always the lessons they had learned as they had put together this wonderful night.

With sadness Meredith thought of the arguments she and Wes had endured as she had taken more and more time away from him to complete the play. She thought about last year's play, when she had been mourning her relationship with Nick, how she had been comforted by Beth. She closed her eyes and wondered if it would always be this way, if she would continue to drift from place to place, every year looking back with longing to the year before. The thought made her that much more eager to marry Shane.

When the play was over and the audience had erupted into applause, once again a senior stood before the microphone and asked Meredith to approach to receive flowers, only this time she was not alone, for Scott was asked to approach, as well.

When the two stood before the audience, Scott turned to Meredith and embraced her, and took her hand; the two waved once more and descended back to their seats, to the applause of their friends.

Afterward, Meredith and Scott met the students backstage to congratulate and thank them, leaving the others in the lobby to chat. They spent a pleasant half hour with their students and then walked toward the lobby again, but not before Scott stopped halfway down the hallway.

"Hold on, Meredith."

Meredith turned and looked at Scott expectantly.

"I just wanted to say thanks."

Meredith smiled. "For what?"

"For everything. You've been a good friend to me this year. I really enjoyed working with you, and I never would have become involved with the drama team had it not been for you." He grinned. "I found a new job, Meredith. I'm not coming back to Dover next year. And guess what," he continued, pointing to himself with both thumbs. "I'm going to be the drama advisor at my new school."

"Oh, Scott, what great news!" Meredith cried, clasping her hands together with joy. "I'm so proud of you!"

"It's all because of you. And I'd also like to say that I appreciate the advice you gave me about proposing to Marianne. I took your advice, and it was perfect."

"I'm so happy for you. You have so many good things coming to you, and you deserve every one of them. Although," she said as she suffered a sharp pang of sorrow, "I'm going to miss you next year." She paused for a second and smiled. "You helped make this a good year for me."

At that moment, several students emerged from the back room, and Meredith and Scott waved and said hello. Meredith recognized Rosalie as part of the group and made a special effort to smile.

"Anyway, you're a special person, Scott, and I'm glad I had the chance to spend time with you this year."

"Likewise."

Scott held out his arms to her and smiled, and she embraced him warmly. They stood like this for a few seconds before separating. Scott put his hands in his pockets and began walking again. Meredith walked beside him, until he stopped again.

"One more thing," he said, his face turning more serious. "I'm sorry you've had a hard time this year. You know, between Wes and Nancy—"

"It's okay, Scott," Meredith interrupted, not wanting to spoil the moment. "All in all it's been a good year."

"Hey, listen," he said tentatively, frowning. "I want you to know that we all support you and are looking forward to your wedding. We just want you to be happy."

"I know. Thank you."

They walked back to the lobby in silence, rejoining the others; they all embraced, said goodbye, and went home.

ON MONDAY, Meredith went to school knowing her seniors had seen their graded essays. Ordinarily she would be nervous about the conversation she was about to have with Jason, but she felt oddly at peace. She didn't know if she was merely convinced that she was doing the right thing, or if she was numb, or if she was suppressing an overwhelming sense of foreboding and had accepted it. But when Jason approached her after class, his face ashen and frightened, she spoke to him with calm confidence, surprised that her heart was beating at its normal speed.

"You wanted to see me," he said quietly after the last student had left.

"Yes," Meredith said, her expression severe but her voice not without softness. "Do you know what this is about?"

"No," said Jason, his forehead scrunching and his face assuming a look of confusion. "Why did I fail the paper? I worked hard on it."

Meredith frowned. "Jason, I want you to look me in the eye and tell me you wrote this paper."

Jason stared at her, his face now red. "I wrote this paper," he told her.

Meredith looked at him for a moment or two. Wordlessly, she cast her eyes downward to her desk, retrieving the highlighted essay she had printed from the internet. She passed it to him without speaking and watched for his reaction.

He took it. As he glanced at it, the light of recognition crossed his face, and his eyes opened wide. His cheeks grew redder, and he continued to look at the paper, avoiding her gaze. Meredith guessed he was trying to decide what to say, how he could get out of this.

"What do you think?" she asked.

Finally he looked at her. "I don't know anything about this."

Meredith cocked her head and frowned. "Don't do this," she said. "If you admit to plagiarizing, I might be willing to work with you. You'll still have to fail the paper, but at least you'd get the chance to rewrite it and bring up your grade. That means you could still pass the class."

"But my record would say that I had plagiarized."

"Yes."

Jason shook his head. "No way." He handed the paper back to her. "I don't know where this essay came from, but there's some sort of weird mix-up."

"I'm going to have to call your parents, Jason."

"I'm sure they'll tell you the same thing. My parents know I wouldn't cheat."

Meredith knew they knew that. Of course they did. She sighed. Nancy would have her head over this, but maybe Jason would learn his lesson. If he did, it would all be worth it.

THAT NIGHT MEREDITH shakily dialed the Richters, but she received no answer. She didn't know if they weren't available or if they were avoiding her call, but she was relieved. She didn't want to deal with them at the moment. She put the number away and packed up her papers, then decided to go to sleep early. She tried to call Shane from bed, but he didn't answer.

The next morning, a receptionist knocked on her classroom door as she was preparing for her first class. The receptionist informed her that she was needed in Nancy's office right away. Meredith thanked the receptionist, placed the book she was holding on her desk, and followed the receptionist toward Nancy's office.

She knocked tentatively and was told to enter. To her great surprise, Nancy was not alone in her office. Also there was Scott, who was already seated in front of Nancy's desk, and Katrina, who was sitting in a chair in the corner, facing Scott. As she entered the room, Meredith was shocked to find Rosalie sitting off to the side, facing Katrina from the other side of the room. She looked at Rosalie, but Rosalie was avoiding her gaze. Meredith looked around the room. There was an ominous presence. She had no idea what this was about, but she knew in her heart what was going to happen.

"Sit down, Meredith," Nancy said tersely, holding her hand toward the chair next to Scott.

Meredith took her seat. Scott glanced at her, but his gaze did not linger. She turned to Nancy, but said nothing.

"Thank you for coming," Nancy said to the room at large. She directed her attention to Meredith and Scott. "You two are here because some serious allegations have arisen. Rumors have surfaced that you have been engaging in an inappropriate relationship on school grounds."

Meredith opened her eyes wide and looked at Katrina. She

knew instantly that Katrina did not want to be here, that she had nothing to do with what Nancy was saying and that she had been backed into a corner. She would not look at Meredith; she was looking down into her lap, where her hands were grasping each other until they were red.

Meredith looked at Scott, whose face, like her own, showed shock and horror. She turned back to Nancy.

"Where are these allegations coming from?" she asked, but suddenly she knew. Furious, she turned around and faced Rosalie.

"Rosalie, what is this about?" she asked, barely controlling her anger. "You know there's nothing going on between Mr. Halloway and me. What are you thinking of?"

"Control your tone," Nancy ordered, and Meredith turned toward her. "Rosalie is only doing what she thinks is right."

"Nancy, you know there has been tension between Rosalie and me this year. You must realize what's going on here."

"I don't know anything until I hear both sides of this story, and I'd appreciate your letting me do that without interruption."

"But this is ridiculous! Scott and I are friends and nothing more. We worked on the play together. Of course we were spending a lot of time together."

"Rosalie tells me she saw some suspicious behavior the night of the play."

Meredith laughed. "If by suspicious you mean a friendly hug after congratulating each other on a job well done, then yes, I suppose she's right," she said. "Nancy, I've had some personal challenges this year, and Scott has been there to support me every step of the way. I love Scott, as a friend. But the idea that there's something else going on, that we'd use the school to have some sort of illicit affair, is just absurd."

"She's right," Scott intervened finally, having recovered from his shock. "Meredith is a good friend, but there's never been anything more than that between us."

Nancy turned to Rosalie. "Is it possible you were mistaken?"

"No," said Rosalie in a clearly rehearsed display of confidence. "I know what I saw."

"Nancy," said Meredith, "there were several other students with Rosalie that night. I'm sure if you question them, you will find that what Rosalie saw simply didn't happen."

Nancy's face iced over, and she turned again to Rosalie. "You didn't tell me that," she said. "Who else was with you, Rosalie?"

Rosalie blanched and rattled off a list of names, which Nancy wrote down. Then she turned back to Rosalie.

"I'll be looking into this, but in the meantime you can go, Rosalie. I'd better not find out that this is your way of trying to get back at Miss Beck for an imagined injury."

Heartened by Nancy's words, Meredith watched as Rosalie stood and wordlessly left the room. After the door closed behind her, Meredith turned back to Nancy, feeling lighter and less anxious.

Nancy was looking between her and Scott. "Frankly, I'm inclined to believe you two, though I'm disappointed that you weren't more discreet. You work in a school. It's unprofessional of you to engage in any behavior that can be misinterpreted. Even if I find that your relationship is nothing more than what you've told me it is, I'd still have to warn you that you've stepped dangerously close to being inappropriate. Next time be more careful."

Neither Meredith nor Scott spoke, each eager to be dismissed so they could end this torture and get on with their day.

"Scott, you can go," Nancy said.

Scott stood and nodded in acknowledgement, then smiled weakly at Meredith and left.

Meredith was preparing to leave as well, having relaxed, but when she looked at Katrina, her anxiety returned. Katrina had not grown any more relieved; in fact she looked more upset than she had before. For the first time she looked at Meredith, and at this point her eyes were clouded by tears. She frowned, firmed up her face, and looked down once again.

"Meredith, there is one more matter I'd like to discuss with you," Nancy said, facing her. "Jason Richter."

Meredith nodded but said nothing, wanting first to know what Nancy had to say.

"I received a call last night from Jason's father. It seems that Jason failed his essay and that you accused him of plagiarizing his paper from an essay he found online."

Meredith fortified herself. "Yes," she said, and swallowed, folding her hands in her lap. "That's right."

Nancy stared at her. "I recall telling you to let Jason rewrite his paper."

"You did. I told him that if he admitted to what he had done, I would give him the opportunity to rewrite his paper."

"Jason says he is going to fail the paper regardless."

"He is. He cheated on that paper. But if he admits to plagiarizing, he can rewrite it just the same for a second grade, in order to pass the class."

Nancy's expression changed imperceptibly as she realized what Meredith had done, that she had found a way to carry out Nancy's request without appearing to go against her wishes. She smirked and nodded.

"I'm not stupid, Meredith, and neither are you. I know what you're doing. You're deliberately going against what I instructed you to do."

"Yes, I am. I'm sorry, Nancy, but you and I are going to have to agree to disagree here. I decided I just couldn't let him get away with another plagiarized paper. He's been swindling us all year, in the process learning that cheating is okay. I have to put a stop to it."

Nancy was studying her in silence. Meredith looked at Katrina. Katrina was watching her, her eyes soft with apology. Then Katrina looked back at Nancy, seeming to brace for what was coming.

"Meredith, you and I have had many differences this year,"

Nancy said. "But I have explicitly told you my feelings on this matter, many times, and you've chosen to take it upon yourself to handle it. As I've said before, I am amazed by how brazen you've been in your insistence that you know best, that you, and not I, have a better understanding of how the school operates and what its needs are. You clearly are not capable of acting for the benefit of the school; it appears that you are more concerned with being right, with carrying out your own agenda."

"Nancy, I—"

"I'm sorry, Meredith, but you're not being asked to return to teach at Dover next year," Nancy concluded. "We're bringing in another teacher to fill your position."

Meredith stared at her, surprised but not shocked. She felt she had always known she would be fired from this job, that Nancy had been looking for reasons to get rid of her and that she eventually would find the perfect opportunity. She nodded numbly as she contemplated what to do now. Once again she would be looking for a job, would have to start over with new friends, new students, and new classes. She looked at Katrina. She was wiping tears from the corners of her eyes.

She turned back to Nancy. "Was there anything else?"

"No. You may go."

Meredith stood, turned toward the door, and left.

She walked back to her classroom. Her first class would start in about five minutes; students were flitting here and there as they gathered their books and strode briskly toward their rooms. As she opened the door to her classroom, she felt a hand on her shoulder and turned. Katrina was standing behind her. Meredith embraced her and felt her friend's arms wrap around her. Meredith separated from her and opened the door to her classroom. Three students were sitting together chatting; they looked up when the teachers entered, surprised by the emotion on their faces.

Meredith said kindly, "Would you mind excusing us for a moment?"

"Sure," said one of the students, and all three rose and walked out, braving curious glances as they did.

Katrina watched them, then faced Meredith once they had left. "Meredith, I'm so sorry," she said tearfully. "I had no idea this was going to happen. Nancy took me totally by surprise this morning. I had no time to warn you."

Meredith took her hand. "Please don't apologize, Katrina. There was nothing you could do. I completely understand."

"I can't believe this bullshit," Katrina spat, wiping her tears. "Nancy is out of control. She had no right to fire you." She sniffled and withdrew a tissue from her purse, then blew her nose and sneered. "She's the one with her own agenda, not you."

Meredith remembered something. "Nancy said they already have another teacher to fill my spot. How is that possible if this just happened?"

"Because the new teacher is Nancy's daughter. She wanted her to have your spot this year, but Kevin Williams talked to the board and convinced them to hire you instead."

Meredith couldn't stop a wry grin from sliding across her face as all the pieces fell into place. "Ah," she said. "Now it all makes sense."

"Meredith, I knew that Nancy wanted her daughter here this year." Katrina's voice shook as she spoke these words. "I was sworn to secrecy; otherwise I would have told you. But I promise you, I would have warned you about today had I known. I had no idea she was capable of this."

"I believe you," Meredith said, and squeezed her friend's hand.

"I wanted to defend you in there," Katrina continued. "And I would put myself in the line of fire if it weren't for Perry. I just can't lose my job, for his sake. It's just that—"

"Katrina, you did nothing wrong. Don't beat yourself up over this." Meredith sighed, withdrew her hand, and smiled. "You did the right thing. You need to look after your son. He needs you more than I need this job."

Katrina calmed herself and looked at Meredith. "You're amazing," she said, shaking her head. "In spite of everything you've been through, you never hold anything against anyone, and you endure it with bravery and a positive attitude." She frowned. "You don't deserve any of it. It's not fair."

"Maybe I do deserve it. Maybe it will lead me to where I need to be." Meredith attempted a smile, trying to convince herself that she believed what she was saying. "In the meantime, I'm very fortunate to have such good friends to help me through it. I'll miss you," she said then, with sorrow. "I can handle what I've been through. What I can't handle are so many goodbyes."

SOMEHOW MEREDITH MADE it through her classes and actually felt more warmly toward her students than ever, knowing she wouldn't be returning to see them next year. She smiled at Rosalie and Jason as if nothing had happened, remembering that they were kids and that one day they would regret what they had done, and not having the energy or the malice to feel angry with them. Also, she could relate to them, having had parents for whom nothing was good enough.

She was particularly sorry that she had not managed to reach Rosalie. As Rosalie worked on a project that day, her head down, dark hair falling over her face, Meredith thought about how childlike she looked, how ill at ease she always seemed to be. She knew Rosalie missed Eliza Chen, Meredith's predecessor, who had taken her under her wing when she'd needed comforting. She had hoped to replace her, to be a safe place for Rosalie, and she couldn't help feeling that she had failed. It was her one regret about her schoolyear, the biggest regret of her career.

During lunch she sat with Henry, Katrina, and Scott, sharing tears and laughter and sighs as they reminisced about the year and said their early goodbyes. They still had one more week of classes, and then exams, before graduation, and they resolved to make the most of the time they had left together.

The day held one ironic bright spot. A colleague who supervised the organization of the yearbook informed Meredith that the seniors had chosen to dedicate the yearbook to her, citing her kindness, honesty, talent, and willingness to help as only some of the many reasons behind their decision. Meredith allowed herself a chuckle. At least those who mattered had appreciated her.

Meredith drove home that day feeling a mixture of relief, shock, and fear. Part of her couldn't believe she had been fired. She had thrived at every other job she had had. She grimaced when she thought about applying for a new job, especially this late in the year. She realized she might not be able to teach next year, and she considered with heightening anxiety how difficult it would be to find a job after a year's hiatus. She had to smile at the irony. Wes had wanted her to quit to be with him, and she had said no. Now she wouldn't be teaching there anyway.

She was thinking of Wes as she pulled onto her street, and she was startled to see him in front of her house as she approached her driveway. He appeared to be walking home from visiting the O'Reillys, and he stopped and waved as she parked her car, then waited as she stepped out, her work bag in hand.

She smiled at him as he walked casually toward her, meeting her on the sidewalk in front of her driveway.

"Hi, Wes," she said. She tried to make her voice upbeat but knew she couldn't possibly hide her emotions from him.

"Hi," he responded, furrowing his brow at her tone. "What's wrong?"

She looked at him and sighed. "I was fired today," she told

him, and relaxed her shoulders, giving in and letting herself feel the sorrow.

Wes's eyes widened at first, then narrowed with sympathy.

"Oh, sweetheart—I'm sorry!" he exclaimed, and opened his arms.

She went to him, infinitely grateful for the comfort. As he embraced her, she abruptly experienced the sensation of falling; being in his arms again, basking in the safety of him, was almost too much for her to bear, and she let her senses consume him as she leaned into his chest. Being so close to him again, she yearned to wrap her arms around him and lift her chin for a kiss. She stepped back nervously, avoiding his gaze, and wiped her eyes on her sleeve, unnerved by the power of her feelings.

She couldn't bear to look at his face; she was staring at the ground by his feet, fearing to let him see her face lest he sense the ambivalence there. She was frightened by her sudden longing for him, feeling irresistibly drawn to the familiarity of him. She thought of how different it was with Shane, and she wondered if she would ever have with him what she had had with Wes.

From above she heard Wes's voice:

"Come on over to my place. I'll fix you a nice dinner."

At these words, she looked upward and met his eyes. His expression was sad but kind, and she knew he was offering his friendship and that she had to take it, for his sake as well as for her own. She smiled and nodded, letting him carry her bag up to her porch for her before he rejoined her on the sidewalk. They walked side by side across the street toward his house, where he held the door for her as she stepped inside.

He strode past her to the kitchen, where he opened the refrigerator and stared, thinking. He then bent down and retrieved two chicken breasts and grabbed various vegetables. As he stepped deftly around the kitchen, deep in thought, Meredith watched him, feeling better by the moment. She smiled through glistening eyes.

"Thanks for having me over, Wes. This is exactly what I needed."

"It's no problem," he said, glancing at her and smiling. He was facing her, standing on the other side of the island, where she sat on a stool, leaning on the counter. Meredith was happy to put her anxiety aside and relax in a place she knew well, a place where she felt safe. During this precious time she was able to forget the events of the last few months and focus on Wes, on the closeness they had had and the bond they had fostered. She soaked in his presence, once again allowing herself to be charmed and swept away by him, relishing how easy he was to talk to.

"I'm happy to have company tonight. I appreciate it very much."

"As I said, it's no problem." He paused while he searched for a knife. "Why don't you tell me what happened? This doesn't by any chance have anything to do with Jason, does it?"

"Good guess," she said, and told him about Jason's essay and her confrontation with Nancy that morning.

He was listening intently, having stopped cooking so he could watch her. When she finished speaking, he folded his arms. "I'm glad you finally were able to catch him in the act," he told her. "Maybe next time he'll think twice before cheating."

"I hope so."

"I'm proud of you, Meredith. You did a difficult thing, but it was the right thing. Not everyone would have the courage to do it." His eyes were fixed on hers. His expression was firm, but it softened as he spoke. "You're an amazing person."

He looked like he wanted to say more, but he was silent. Meredith felt color rise to her face and warmth tumble in her chest. "Thank you," she said quietly, embarrassed. "I just did what had to be done."

He was staring at her, in consideration. Finally, he said, "I feel truly privileged to have gotten to know you." He swallowed, then forced a dazzling smile onto his face. "There. How's that for sappy?"

"I love it," she said, returning his smile, grateful to him for lightening the mood. "The feeling is mutual."

His dazzling smile had turned warm and sincere. He leaned across the countertop and placed his hand on hers, letting it linger for several moments before patting it lightly in a sympathetic gesture that made Meredith's heart leap.

"I didn't tell you the whole story," she said slyly. "Rosalie was there. She accused Scott and me of having an affair."

Wes raised his eyebrows as he placed the chicken onto a sizzling skillet. "Is that right?" he said, casting her a quick glance before reaching across the countertop to grab a pair of tongs. "And whatever would have given her that impression?"

"She saw us in a hug the night of the play. We were thanking each other for our friendship this year."

"You and Scott never did make a secret of the fact that you enjoyed each other's company," said Wes, stopping for a moment to rest his hands on the countertop and study her. "But Rosalie should have kept her mouth shut."

"I guess she thought she was doing the right thing."

"I should have kept my mouth shut too."

Meredith looked at him, surprised. "What do you mean?"

"I mean just what I said. I regret giving you a hard time about Scott. It was childish and disrespectful. I'm sorry."

Meredith couldn't take her eyes off him; he was still staring at her, trying to impart his sincerity through the intensity of his gaze. She sighed, smiled, and cupped her chin in her hand, her elbow on the countertop. "It's okay," she said, picking a slice of red pepper off a plate. "I could have been more understanding too."

"I guess that makes us even."

She lifted her face and looked at him again, and her smile widened. "I guess it does."

They spent the evening in this fashion, enjoying Wes's dinner and chatting casually. Meredith asked Wes about work and told him about the success of the school play. Her heart ached when Wes updated her on Helen's pregnancy; she was due in a few months, with a little girl, to be named Olivia Ethel. Meredith inquired after Sarah and listened with joy, in the back of her mind lamenting that from now on the mother-in-law she'd inquire after would be Tess.

Eventually darkness fell, and Meredith grew tired. The conversation lulled, and they sat awkwardly, neither knowing what to do next.

Meredith sighed once more and stood. "Well, I'd better be going. I may be fired, but I do have to finish out the year, and I have work to do at home." She picked up her plate and glass to bring them to the sink.

"I'll get that," he said, pressing her hand gently back to the countertop.

He left his hand on hers and faced her, his expression serious, his lips drawn out into a thoughtful line. Meredith could see his chest heaving; his eyes widened as he watched her, and Meredith could almost sense him deciding whether he should step closer toward her or let her go.

She was once again afraid to look at his face, but she did, slowly lifting her eyes to meet his. When she did, she wished she hadn't, for she was instantly pulled into him, as she always was, enchanted by the softness of his handsome features. She didn't know how it happened, but suddenly they were standing mere inches apart; his hand was drifting toward her waist and then was on her, and the feel of his hand on her hip set her on fire.

"Meredith," he whispered, bringing his other hand to her cheek and brushing his fingers tenderly over her neck.

She felt her eyes closing and her lips parting, sensed her chin lifting toward his and her arms reaching for him. All at once she stopped and pulled away, forcing herself to take one step back, breaking the spell. She opened her eyes and looked at him. His brow was furrowed with hope, disbelief, and desire, as if he had been imagining this moment since their breakup and couldn't believe he was fortunate enough that the vision was coming true. Meredith hated to steal it from him, but she knew if she submitted she would end up in the same place from which she had just escaped; she had been there before, and she knew that as much as she adored him, her future did not lie with him. A kiss with Wes, a renewal of their romance, would feel blissful now but would leave her broken in the end, and she resisted, alight with need as she was.

She exhaled sharply, closing her eyes to regain her composure, and he himself took a few reluctant steps back, closing his lips and inhaling, trying to shake off his lapse of control.

She felt she had to say something.

"Wes—" she began, but she was interrupted.

"It doesn't have to be this way," he told her, his voice low and even, but gentle. "There's still time. He'll be sad for a day or two, but he'll get over it." Here he approached her again and held her shoulders in his hands, and Meredith ached to fall into him once more. "But I love you, sweetheart. I'll be good to you forever."

Meredith closed her eyes slowly, then opened them, knowing they held her answer and wishing it were as simple as he made it sound.

Suddenly she pressed her hands to his face and kissed him with passion, then stepped back, her expression heavy with love and sorrow.

"Thank you for tonight, Wes," she said, her voice a hoarse whisper. She took several steps backward, watching him drift further away from her, his expression turning more and more longing with each step she took. "I won't forget what you've done for me."

She turned and left quickly, before she could change her mind, before she could surrender.

CHAPTER ELEVEN

LOOKING FORWARD

*E*xam week flew by in a blur, and graduation came and went. Meredith had an emotional day signing yearbooks and saying goodbye to students and colleagues. She made sure to have a photograph taken of herself with Henry, Katrina, and Scott. Their friendships had been the high point of her school year, and she left them tearfully, promising to keep in touch. She would see them at her wedding in a few days but knew she would have very little time to talk to them then.

She went to sleep that night heavy-hearted. She had no job lined up for next year and no place to live. She would have Frank and Grace's house until the end of July; then she would need to move, unless she wished to buy it—otherwise they needed to put it on the market or rent it out to someone who would take it off their hands. Her marriage to Shane was the only stable part of her life. The thought made her uneasy.

Graduation took place on Wednesday. First thing Thursday morning, Meredith would grab her suitcases and head out to Frederick, where she would stay with the Thayers until her wedding on Saturday. Sunday morning she and Shane would fly out to Hawaii for a two-week honeymoon. Meredith was looking forward to the honeymoon for many reasons but was nervous about getting through the wedding first. There seemed to be too many things that could go wrong. She longed for the moment when she would be settled, when she would know where she was going. Saturday afternoon she would know. The idea comforted her, and her mind drifted back to it whenever she grew nervous.

Meredith had agonized over who on her side to invite and had decided on very few people. Tara of course would be there with her family; she was Meredith's matron of honor. Henry, Katrina, and Scott would be there with their significant others. Meredith had wondered whether to invite any of her neighbors. Ultimately she had decided not to. She had a feeling they would understand.

Her parents would be there, as would Vince. Her father had agreed to walk her down the aisle, though he had not been happy about it. Meredith had spoken with her father more in the last two weeks than she had in the last two years; he had called her repeatedly, asking for details and trying to talk her out of what he saw as the biggest mistake of her life. He had begged her to back out, telling her he knew a multitude of eligible bachelors and that if she was so desperate to marry the son of a senator he simply had to take out his address book to find her someone more suitable. Meredith had tried to ignore him. Finally the Becks had accepted the fact that Meredith was unyielding and had decided to make the most of it, as had the Thayers.

Meredith's guest list had nearly stopped there. Her parents had added a few obligatory relatives, but they were not treating this as the grand affair they had hoped they would have for their daughter. When Tess saw her list, she looked at Meredith with surprise, and possibly pity—Meredith wasn't sure. Meredith had explained to Tess that she desired a small, intimate wedding. The Thayers and the Becks had been all too happy to oblige. Meredith knew that her mother and Tess had been in contact several times and that they had been cold but cordial. Each was pleased that they needn't invite the multitudes to witness an event that nobody saw as a reason to celebrate. The Thayers had kept their list short, as well—longer by far than Meredith's but much simpler than it would have been otherwise.

There was one exception. Meredith had decided, after much thought, to invite Adam's parents, Will and Cynthia Quinn, and his siblings Erin and Andrew. She hadn't been in contact with them since the months after Adam passed away, but something told her to invite them anyway. Their note accepting her invitation had been warm and excited. She longed to see them but was anxious, as well. In order to embrace the future, she had avoided thinking of the past. She wasn't sure what would happen when her past and her future collided.

Lying in bed that night, staring up at the ceiling, not feeling the slightest bit tired, Meredith reflected on the year she had lived in that house. That night would be the last night she would spend there. After their honeymoon, she and Shane would live together in his townhouse for a few weeks until they closed on the house the Thayers had helped him secure. Meredith had spent the last couple of weeks packing up her few belongings and bringing her books back into the living room in preparation for the move. When their house was ready, she would return to retrieve them. Until then they would sit here, waiting. Meredith took comfort in the fact that she finally would be able to unpack her books, to have a place for them. She looked forward to being surrounded by them once again.

It was hard to believe she had been there nearly a year. She remembered the first night she had spent there, how she had explored the house, wondering what her life would be like. She had enjoyed meeting her neighbors and ultimately Wes, who would come to define her time there and who would bring meaning to it. She thought of the many times she had crossed the street to be with him, how his presence there had been her rock. Their separation had inspired her to redefine what she was looking for in her life, had changed her expectations and driven her to Shane. Once again she looked back on a year and realized how different a person she had become.

She wondered how her life had become so complicated. She had hoped to avoid complexity and drama, and here she was embroiled in what nearly amounted to a family feud. The irony was that the more complex the situation had become, the more she knew she had to keep going; there came a point when she was so entangled that to extract herself would cause more chaos than following through with her plans. So she sprinted toward the end, toward the conclusion for which she longed so she could handle known challenges with open eyes.

With this mindset she managed to drift off to sleep, awakening before the sun rose so she could load her suitcases into her car and drive to Frederick, only to return later as Shane's wife. Her heart was pounding in her chest as, under the cover of the darkness of early morning, she quietly climbed into her car and sat for a moment looking at her house, then pulled out of the driveway toward her final destination. She glanced at Wes's house as she drove away, imagining him inside and deliberately pushing forward. She didn't know if the tears that fell were tears of sorrow or of relief.

MEREDITH WAS to spend Thursday with Shane and the Thayers, making last minute decisions and checking up on the finer details of the wedding, though she felt strangely separated from it all, as Tess and Maribel had made many decisions without her. Meredith was surprised to find, for example, that the centerpieces had been changed from her original idea and that she and Shane would spend their wedding night not in the bridal suite at the country club, as she had assumed, but rather in a hotel nearby, where they would meet their families for breakfast before leaving for their honeymoon. These changes irritated Meredith but were merely background noise in an already chaotic weekend. She had much bigger concerns than flowers and hotels, and she accepted these surprises without complaint.

Friday night her parents and Vince would arrive, Vince having flown to Philadelphia so they could drive down together. Tara and her family would arrive the same night, and this was the event to which Meredith most looked forward. She knew she would feel better once she was with Tara. That night would be the rehearsal and the dinner. Tara would stay with her at the Thayers' house that night, leaving Tom and the girls at their room in the hotel. Saturday morning, Meredith and Shane would be married.

When Meredith arrived at the Thayers' home on Thursday morning, she was relieved to see Shane's car already in the driveway. She removed her suitcases from the car and dragged them up to the door, where she rang the bell and waited for a long time before the door was opened by Roger, who courteously escorted her inside and brought her bags upstairs. A moment later he descended the staircase with Shane, deep in conversation. Shane's eyes met hers as he reached the bottom step, and as Roger separated from him and excused himself, Shane stepped toward her and smiled.

"Hey," he said as he kissed her. "We're getting married this weekend."

"So I've heard," she responded, grinning.

"Not from my parents, I'll bet," he replied with an irritated grimace. "They seem to just want to get this over with, and with as few people knowing as humanly possible. You'd think they'd be happy for me," he said, more to himself than to her. "I guess they're mad because I'm actually doing something on my own this time. God forbid I don't beg permission from the almighty senator."

"Well," Meredith said, patting his arm, "at least we'll be married in a couple of days." She put on her kindest smile. "Then we can just enjoy our honeymoon, without anyone's disapproval or criticism."

"Yeah," said Shane, and he sneered. "I'm just glad I can finally show them that they can't control my life. Maybe now they'll let up and leave me alone."

Meredith stared at him. "And, it will be nice to be together," she said, her voice touched with sarcasm.

Shane shook off his dark thoughts and looked at her. "Definitely," he said silkily, with a sly grin, slipping his hands around her waist. His face turned more serious then, and he gently touched her hair, running his fingers through it. "I'm sorry," he said, closing his eyes and shaking his head for a moment before looking at her once more. "My parents are being awful, as always. I hate that they're acting like this is a catastrophe. But I'm looking forward to being with you," he said, and smiled. "Hey," he added, his face turning earnest. "Thanks for marrying me. It's nice to know at least one person has faith in me."

At that moment they were interrupted by Maribel, who burst through the front door with a wide smile, followed by Peter, looking stoic and saying nothing, as always.

"Look who it is!" Maribel exclaimed, holding out her arms to Meredith. "In a couple of days we'll be family."

"I can't wait," Meredith replied pleasantly, embracing her.

Maribel drew Meredith away as she began discussing details and asking for Meredith's opinions. As she was led into the kitchen, Meredith turned her head back toward Shane, intending to shoot him a smile in parting. He was standing there sulkily with Peter. Neither man was speaking; each was standing with his hands in his pockets, looking down at the floor, deep in his own thoughts.

⌇

MEREDITH SAW little of Tess that day and wasn't sorry about it. She felt that the less she saw her future mother-in-law before the wedding, the less chance there was of something going wrong. She spent most of her time with Maribel, hoping to see more of Shane but knowing the hustle and bustle was necessary, and letting Maribel shuffle her around the house and out to visit with vendors, finalizing the details. She wasn't even sure what Shane was doing most of the day; though she saw him occasionally in passing, he stepped out midday and didn't return until dinner. Meredith assumed that, seeing as he wasn't needed, he sought some fresh air, and she couldn't blame him. She wished she could spend some time by herself, as well.

That night Shane took Meredith's hand and led her to his car, and the two of them grabbed a pizza. They ate in silence, enjoying some peace after the hubbub of the day's planning. After they returned to the Thayers' house, when they had reached the front door, Shane held her back, his hand on her shoulder, and kissed her. When he pulled away, he continued to hold her tight, and looked at her, his eyes dark, his lips touched with a lustful smile.

"Hey," he whispered hoarsely, nudging her as he held her, and grinning. "Why don't you let me stay with you tonight? Come on, it'll be fun." He slid his hand under her shirt, hoping to persuade her.

"Shane, we have only two more nights. Just wait until after the wedding. The anticipation will make it better, in my opinion."

"Mmm," he breathed, kissing her neck and squeezing her. "Fine, I guess, but if that's your argument, waiting seems kind of unnecessary. It would be amazing even without the anticipation."

He was tickling her, and she giggled. "I'm sorry. I know it's not easy. Thanks for being so patient." She kissed him and slid her hands up and down his chest. "I'm looking forward to the wedding night. I know it will be amazing."

"Yeah," he said, a little absentmindedly. He returned her kiss and pushed away from her, and sighed. "Well, even though you're torturing me, I admire your fortitude. You definitely follow through when you say you're going to do something. I kind of wish you weren't so strong."

"I do too, sometimes," she laughed. She held out her hand. "Are you coming inside?"

"Nah, I think I'll go for a drive," he told her, looking back at his car and jingling his keys. He raised his eyebrows as he looked at her. "Is that cool with you?"

"Sure," she said, disappointed, her smile fading a little. "Is everything okay?"

"Yeah, fine," he said pleasantly, stepping backward. "I'll see you tomorrow." He turned and walked toward his car. "Later, babe," he added over his shoulder.

Meredith watched him climb into his car, feeling happy. She wished Shane would stay, but she had been delighted by his mood. She stepped inside and up to bed, her mind busy and her heart fluttering. The following day, she would see her parents again, as well as her brother and Tara. She was nervous about how they would interact with her future family. In a day and a half, she would be married. As she drifted off to sleep, she began to remember the journey that had brought her here, but she wasn't in the mood to think so deeply and put it out of her mind, instead choosing to imagine her wedding night with Shane. She smiled with anticipation. She had a feeling she would be pleasantly surprised. She sighed as she envisioned his strong, brawny body unclothed. At least she had one thing to look forward to.

MEREDITH FELT ALMOST as anxious about Friday as she did about Saturday. She woke up several times Thursday night, eager to get the day started already, and rose just after six o'clock to shower and dress. She found herself sitting in silence in the kitchen, however, with an untouched cup of coffee and nothing to do. It would be hours before any of her family would arrive.

The Thayers began to rise and descend from their rooms at around eight o'clock. They nodded to her in acknowledgement. Meredith thought glumly that anyone looking in on the situation would have no idea that a wedding was taking place that weekend. But she trudged on, reminding herself that she wasn't doing this for a big wedding or great excitement. As long as she emerged from the weekend married and secure, and free of the Thayers for at least two weeks, she would be happy.

Finally it was time to dress for the rehearsal and the dinner, which would take place at the country club. At this point Meredith began to feel dizzy; her parents would be face to face with the Thayers in less than two hours. The thought horrified her. She had no idea what was going to happen.

She and Shane climbed into his car that afternoon and headed over to the club. Meredith was wearing a pale pink dress, with her hair down and pushed back into a tortoise shell headband. Shane looked especially handsome, she thought, in dressy camel-colored slacks, a white dress shirt, and a pink tie. A navy sports jacket hung from a hook in the backseat.

"I'm so nervous," she couldn't help saying as he pulled out of the driveway.

"Just remember that the day after tomorrow we'll be lying on a beach drinking mai tais," he said as he backed out, his hand on her headrest. "They can all go to hell."

They drove in silence for several minutes.

"Does your life look the way you thought it would look?" Meredith asked him suddenly, not really knowing why.

He was quiet for a few moments, then frowned with consideration. "I don't know. I guess? I wasn't on any kind of timeline, if that's what you mean."

Meredith couldn't think of a response, and said nothing.

"What about you?" he asked, turning to her briefly. "You probably had a strict timeline. You seem like a planner."

"It isn't that I had a timeline, necessarily," she said, leaning back in her seat. "I just wanted to have some stability, to feel secure."

"And you chose me to feel secure with? Maybe we should stop at a doctor's office before going to the club. I want to get you checked out."

Meredith wasn't sure whether to laugh. She might have, had her heart not been steadily sinking all day. She turned away from him and looked out the window, hoping to distract herself from her dark thoughts.

MEREDITH HAD to admit that the club looked beautiful, and her spirits rose marginally as she witnessed workers setting up for her wedding. At least the pictures would look nice. Maybe by the time she and Shane had children, they would be blissfully in love and could tell them it had always been so.

Shane's mood seemed lifted too, and he was affectionate with her, holding her hand and kissing her, despite scornful looks from his parents and Roger. Meredith was further encouraged not only by Shane's loving behavior but also by the fact that she was excited by it. She was happy to be reminded that in fact she and Shane did have warm feelings toward each other and had now been together for several months. In the chaos of the last few weeks, she had nearly forgotten.

Meredith thought her heart would burst with joy when the doors opened and she spotted Tara, standing beside Tom and just behind the girls, who wore matching floral dresses and had their hair tied into pigtails with pink bows. Meredith ran to her and, with a wide smile, took her hand.

"I am so glad you're here. I'm so glad Tom is here. I'm so glad the girls are here. Thank you for bringing them. They shed light on the entire weekend."

"Are you kidding? They wouldn't miss it. Evelyn is into brides now. She can't wait to see Aunt Merry all prettied up in her fancy dress."

Meredith bent down to Evelyn and kissed her cheek. "You get to wear a fancy dress, too. I'll bet you look so beautiful in it."

"It's my princess dress," Evelyn said proudly. "That's what Mommy said."

Tom congratulated Meredith, and Meredith thanked him, happy to see his friendly face. She hugged the girls to her, reveling in their giggles and playfulness, remembering all the good things in her life and feeling more optimistic with every moment.

Meredith picked up Ginger and led Tara, Evelyn, and Tom around the club to show them what was being done. She also introduced them to the Thayers, no longer intimidated now that Tara was there to give her strength. Soon Tom took the girls to the hotel, leaving Tara behind, first transferring Tara's suitcase to Shane's car. Tara kissed him and the girls goodbye and told them she would see them tomorrow at Aunt Merry's wedding. Meredith watched the tender scene with longing, then averted her eyes, giving them privacy.

Meredith felt confident and at ease with Tara by her side, and Tara never left her side, commenting on pretty details and whispering snide observations about the Thayers. Meredith was glad to have someone with whom to share these little thoughts. She appreciated Tara's validating her feelings that Tess was deliberately cruel to her.

"Tess," Meredith said sweetly, placing her hand on her future mother-in-law's shoulder, "Shane tells me you grew up in New Jersey. Tara's mother is from Teaneck. Do you know where that is?"

"Yes," said Tess, glancing at them and folding her arms, then turning away to find Maribel. "I know where that is."

Tara leaned in toward Meredith as Tess walked away. "Where does she get off?" she whispered, her voice heavy with disgust. "Who the hell does she think she is?"

"Senator Thayer's wife."

"And who the hell is Senator Thayer? Just some smartass with strong opinions, like everyone else."

"Speaking of which," Meredith said, sucking in her breath and nodding toward the door.

Meredith felt her stomach lurch as she watched her parents and brother step into the club and look around. Meredith hadn't seen her parents since Labor Day, but they hadn't changed much; they were of equal height, her father looking slim but indomitable, his once dark hair heavily sprinkled with gray. In a plaid blazer, tan slacks, and bowtie, and sporting his round glasses, he looked every bit the intellectual Meredith had always imagined him to be. Her mother looked equally formidable in a flowing black skirt and gray sweater that hugged her graceful figure. Her chin-length hair was set in a neat bob, somehow making her features appear sharper. Their expressions were hesitant but not angry, and from this small fact Meredith found a little hope.

Vince looked dashing in gray slacks and a white dress shirt and tie; he was wearing his hair a bit longer again, and it spiked in all directions without looking messy. Meredith grinned when she saw him. He spotted her across the room and returned her smile; he pointed her out to his parents, and they all approached each other, Meredith and Vince with joy, Harold and Patricia more tentatively.

"Oh, Vince," Meredith exclaimed as they embraced. "I can't tell you how happy I am to see you."

"I'm happy to see you too, and I'm happy to be here," he said, a little loudly; Meredith guessed it was for the benefit of everyone present. He gazed at her with intensity, his eyes sparkling. "I can't believe my little sister is getting married. It's almost too much for me," he said, and Meredith thought he was joking until she saw a tear trying to escape the corner of his eye.

Touched, she wrapped her arm around his waist and pulled him close. "Thanks for being such a great big brother," she said, and smiled up at him. "I've always been able to count on you."

"Not always," he said, his expression growing more serious. He placed his hands on her shoulders. "But I'm trying now."

Meredith was distracted by her parents, who were looking at her with unreadable expressions. They were frowning, almost as if they had synchronized their faces, but the wideness of their eyes made them look almost approachable, as well.

"Hi, Mom. Hi, Dad," she said, embracing them. "Thank you for coming. I really appreciate it."

Harold's eyes were round and thoughtful. "Oh, Meredith," he said, shaking his head. "What the hell are you doing here?" His words were chastising, but his face was touched with softness. "Are you sure you want to do this?"

Meredith nodded, swallowing back tears. "Yes, I am."

Harold sighed. "Well, then, we're here to support you." He threw his hand toward Patricia in a brusque gesture. He turned once more to Meredith. "I suppose it's okay to be headstrong," he said, attempting to joke with her. "There are worse things a person could be."

As he said these words, his eyes drifted over Meredith's shoulder, and he frowned in earnest now, emitting a sound that was something like a growl. Meredith turned and saw Senator Thayer approaching. Her heart thumped in her chest. She searched the room for Shane, but he was nowhere to be found.

Senator Thayer was upon them, walking toward the Becks with his hand extended and his face almost frighteningly bright with a grand smile. "Harold and Patricia," he boomed. Meredith's parents accepted the senator's handshake, which was exaggerated in its forcefulness. "It's a pleasure to see you. What do you think of these kids getting married?"

Harold and Patricia exchanged glances. Patricia said, "We think it's absurd. We've been trying to talk sense into Meredith ever since we found out." She cast Meredith a knowing look. "And you, Senator? We're probably not your first choice for in-laws." Her face broke into a humorless grin.

"No, you're not," said Senator Thayer. "But Meredith's a nice girl, and Shane seems to like her." He shot Meredith a sly look, then turned back to her parents. He held out his arms. "So what do you say? Should we give it a go?"

Harold and Patricia glanced at each other again and shrugged. "What the hell," said Harold. "Let's make life interesting. Let's be in-laws."

Meredith was so relieved she felt as if she could fly. Tara's hand found hers and squeezed, and as Senator Thayer led the Becks around the country club, Meredith wondered if perhaps she might be destined for happiness after all.

THE REHEARSAL and the dinner that followed were surprisingly painless, with the families behaving civilly, if coolly, accepting a less than ideal situation with the most grace they could muster. Meredith's parents were cordial with Shane, congratulating him and thanking him for his parents' hospitality toward their daughter. Shane and Vince chatted, renewing the easy relationship they had begun developing during Vince's visit. Meredith was overjoyed. This lukewarm reception of each other was more than she had hoped for. She was happy that nobody was fighting, that they seemed willing to come to terms with the marriage and that the future wasn't looking as bleak as it had that morning.

At the end of the evening, Meredith, Shane, and Tara piled into Shane's car and headed back to the Thayers' house, where Shane would leave them and return to his townhouse for the night. Roger would be staying with him, and the two would head over to the club the following morning.

Back at the house, Tara walked to the front door and waited politely out of earshot while Meredith and Shane said goodbye for the night. They stood by his car, Shane leaning against the side and holding Meredith's waist as they kissed for the last time before their wedding.

"I can't believe tomorrow is the big day," Meredith said, shaking her head. "It's really here."

"Mmm," said Shane.

"Are you excited?"

"Yeah," he said. "Yeah, I'm excited."

Meredith watched him, trying to discern his tone. His fingers began stroking her skin, not lustfully but lovingly, and his eyes fell to the ground, avoiding her gaze.

"What is it, Shane?"

He looked at her then. "I love you," he said.

Meredith felt her heart melt, her entire body tingling. "You do?"

"Yes," he told her, his eyes round with sincerity. "You're the nicest person I know. I just can't believe you're stupid enough to marry me." He smiled. "I don't know why you're trusting me with your happiness, Meredith, but I want to try to be good to you. I hope I can do it."

"Oh, Shane, I think you can. I know you can." The words burst from her as she was unable to contain her joy. "I love you too," she told him, though she didn't know if she did, and deep down knew she didn't—but she wanted to, and thought she could, and was ready to spend her life trying to do so. His confession changed their entire relationship, as well as her perception of their future together. Suddenly there was a possibility for true partnership, for the kind of relationship she always dreamed for herself, and had had, three times, and watched fall apart. She took his waist in her hands and held him, wishing she could fast forward a day and put the awkwardness of the wedding behind them, to simply be with him, to begin the rest of her life with him, getting to know him and taking her time, without the pressure of uncertainty.

Shane brought his hands to her face, and they met in a kiss. Her hands rested on his chest, then slid to the back of his neck, pulling him closer.

They separated slowly, soft smiles on their faces.

"Well," Shane said, checking the time on his cell phone, "I'd better go."

"Why? Do you have a hot date?" Meredith asked, laughing.

"Yeah, right," he said, and kissed her again.

They wished each other goodnight, and Shane waved to her as he drove away. Meredith watched him go, thinking that the next time she saw him, she would be looking at him from down the aisle.

MEREDITH AND TARA lay in the bed in Meredith's room. They were on their backs, eyes on the ceiling, talking, as they used to when they had sleepovers in high school.

"I will say this, Merry. He is good-looking," Tara was saying. "You're going to have fun tomorrow night." Meredith could hear the grin in Tara's voice. "I can't wait to hear all about it."

"I'll be sure to give you all the details, as always," Meredith replied. "You and your details. You always have to know everything."

"Just you wait," said Tara. "You're going to be married soon. I hate to break it to you, honey, but you won't be on your honeymoon forever. It gets old."

"Let me at least get through my honeymoon before hearing the sad truth. Then we can talk about it all you want."

"Fair enough."

They were silent for a moment.

"Tara," said Meredith finally, "do you think I'm doing the right thing?"

"Honestly, I just don't know." Tara sighed. "I'd like to see you a little more into him, but if I were you I'd probably do the same thing."

"I think everything is going to work out. I couldn't believe how well everyone got along tonight."

"Do you love him, Merry?"

Meredith hesitated. She knew she couldn't lie to Tara. "No," she said. "But I think I can."

"Does he love you?"

"I don't know. He says he does."

Tara turned her head to look at Meredith in the darkness. "I've told you before I'd prefer that you hold out for something better. I think you're worth it. And I think you'd find it. But as long as your mind is made up, I think it could be worse. And Merry," she said, and took her hand. "I'm here for you, no matter what happens."

"I know," said Meredith. "You're the one person who always is."

They were silent, then, for the rest of the night. They fell asleep deep in thought, resolved to wake up the next morning and get Meredith married.

CHAPTER TWELVE

A WEDDING

*M*eredith opened her eyes. The first thing she noticed was that it was a bright, sunny, cheerful day. She turned to look at Tara. Tara was still asleep. Meredith looked back up to the ceiling, taking advantage of the last minutes she'd have before the commotion of the day.

She was getting married in just a few hours. Three years ago she thought she'd be marrying Adam. She thought about how far she had come since then, how different were the circumstances now than they were back then. With Adam everything had seemed ideal. They had had the perfect relationship, the perfect life, and the perfect plans. In contrast, Shane and Meredith were in an odd state of half-love, in which neither was certain of the future but was willing to give it a try. Meredith realized how her perspective had changed since she had been with Adam. She was wiser now; she wasn't expecting perfection anymore. Outside forces could disrupt one's plans at any time, and people's mistakes and insecurities affected lives forever. Life seemed much more complex now. Meredith wondered if it truly was more complex now that Adam was gone or whether it always had been like this, but she had never known it.

She turned toward Tara. She wondered if she would ever have with Shane what Tara had with Tom. Shane was an unlikely and unexpected companion. But the most important lesson Meredith had learned was that one never knew what the future would bring; one never could predict the motives in another person's heart, no matter how close—and that thought gave Meredith hope. Perhaps of all the men in her life, Shane would be the most dependable even though he seemed the least. Meredith had learned never to be surprised. People did unpredictable things all the time.

She missed Adam, but she grew troubled when she thought of Nick and Wes. Adam was no longer with her, but Nick and Wes were alive and well somewhere, probably thinking of her at that very moment. Wes knew she was getting married that day; Meredith imagined him sitting in his kitchen trying not to think about it, and her heart ached for him. She had no doubt that Vince had told Nick that he was flying down for her wedding that weekend, and she thought of him in his own kitchen in Maine, and wondered whether he felt any regret.

But she was marrying Shane, and she had come to terms with the life she had chosen for herself. Maybe with Nick and Wes she had been too naive. She had thought her relationship with Shane was simple—but maybe it was the most complex of all her relationships, the most real. Maybe it would be the one that held the answers.

Tara stirred. She stretched her arms up and opened her eyes.

"Morning," she said.

"Morning."

"It looks like a nice day outside."

"It is."

"Are you ready?"

"Yes."

"Then come on," Tara said, sitting, and patting Meredith's hand. "Let's get up and get you hitched."

MEREDITH AND TARA, along with Maribel, Patricia, and Tess, spent the morning having their hair and makeup done in Meredith's bridal room at the country club. The atmosphere was cool but comfortable; everyone was too busy to remember that few of them liked each other. The necessity of preparation joined them, the way women are often joined under the duress of being pressed for time; they worked together, passing shoes and lipstick and holding each other's clothing as they changed into their wedding attire. Meredith tried not to think too hard this morning. She focused on the details that would make her as beautiful as possible for Shane. She wanted to start her marriage looking perfect.

The ceremony would begin at eleven o'clock. About halfway through the morning, there was a knock at the door. Meredith was just finishing having her hair done and was in her bathrobe, waiting to slip into her dress until the ceremony drew closer. Tara went to the door and opened it a crack, then gasped and opened it wider when she saw who it was.

Cynthia Quinn stepped into the room, and her eyes fell on Meredith. She brought her hands to her face, covering her mouth, and wept. As Meredith rose, already weeping and thankful that she had not yet had her makeup done, Cynthia took her hands from her face and extended her arms to Meredith, who went to her quickly and embraced her with love. They held each other for some time before Cynthia pulled herself away and looked at Meredith, a smile on her lips and in her eyes.

"Meredith, you look so beautiful," she said, shaking her head. "I'm so happy to see you after all this time. Thank you so much for inviting us. We are so honored to be here."

"Oh, Cynthia, it means so much to me that you're here," Meredith told her, breathless as she remembered how much Adam had looked like his mother. "I've thought about you so many times. I've truly missed you," she said, and stopped, for her voice was breaking.

Both women wiped their eyes, momentarily silent.

Meredith lifted her head and sniffled, stifling her tears. "Cynthia, please let me introduce you to my in-laws," she said, extending her arm to Maribel and Tess. "This is Maribel, Shane's sister, and Tess, his mother. Maribel and Tess, this is Cynthia Quinn, Adam's mother."

Maribel and Tess stared at Cynthia.

Tess said coolly, "It's a pleasure to meet you, Cynthia." She turned to Meredith. "Who's Adam?"

Meredith was horrified. She was mortified for Cynthia and embarrassed on her own behalf. She was surprised that Shane had not mentioned to his family that she had been engaged. She and Shane had not discussed Adam at length, but he knew the story; Meredith had made a point of being upfront with him.

She said softly, "Adam was my fiancé."

Tess's eyebrows rose higher, and she threw her head back. "Shane never mentioned to me that you had been engaged," she said.

"My son passed away two and a half years ago," said Cynthia. "That's why he and Meredith weren't married."

Tess's face registered the shock. "My dear, I'm very sorry," she whispered to Cynthia, her expression becoming more gentle than Meredith had ever seen it. She was moved by the change in Tess and guessed her heart broke, having two sons of her own, to imagine the pain Cynthia had endured.

"Thank you," Cynthia said, and turned to Meredith. She took her hands. "Meredith, Will and I just want to tell you that Adam is smiling down on you today. We know he wants you to be happy." She choked on her tears and paused for a moment before continuing. "You are such a special person, and we always knew you would find love again. We're overjoyed that what Adam never had a chance to give you, Shane will." She squeezed Meredith's hands tightly. "We always felt as if you were our daughter, and we've worried about you. Now that you have Shane to love you like Adam loved you, we can stop worrying."

Meredith felt dizzy, but she managed to thank Cynthia as she wished Meredith well once more and left her to finish her preparations. Meredith stood by the door, dumbstruck. She realized she had been staring at the floor and looked up, only to find Tara watching her, her face dark. Meredith turned toward the mirror and looked at herself. She was frowning. She shook off the cloud that had overtaken her mood and forced herself to smile. Soon it would be time to put on her dress. There was no time for reflection.

TARA HELPED MEREDITH GET DRESSED. Tara herself looked stunning, her auburn hair now piled gracefully on top of her head, showing off her long neck and wide round eyes. She was wearing the champagne-colored dress Meredith had chosen for her and Maribel. Meredith watched herself in the mirror as she slid into her own dress, Tara holding various parts of it as Meredith's limbs filled it out. Maribel helped her zip it up, and the three women stood in front of the mirror to admire the bride.

Tess and Patricia joined them by the mirror, and they all stood there, speech eluding them.

Tara was in tears. She placed her hand on Meredith's shoulder. "Merry, you're breathtaking. You deserve all the happiness in the world, honey. And I'm happy for you." She kissed her cheek.

"She's right," said Maribel. "Shane is a very lucky man. And I'm lucky too," she added, kissing Meredith's other cheek.

They turned back toward the mirror and looked at themselves and at each other. Meredith was overwhelmed. She stood there silently as the other women spoke among themselves and backed away toward the other end of the room, and studied herself, thinking about her life, her past and her future. Her mind was remarkably blank. Now she had nothing to do but wait until it was time. She turned toward her family. They were chatting quietly in a corner, making small talk. It was surreal, and Meredith didn't know what to make of it. She thought of Shane, and she brightened. She wondered what he was doing at that moment. She grew excited. She had made it. It was really happening. She breathed a sigh of relief, finally, after all this time, feeling as if she had an answer. She relaxed, knowing now for certain that she'd never feel lost again.

It was just after ten o'clock. Meredith was alone in her room with Tara; Tess, Patricia, and Maribel had left to make sure the men were running on schedule. The two friends were sitting facing each other by the window, enjoying a moment of peace before the excitement of the ceremony.

They were startled by eager knocking at the door. Tara stood to answer it, Meredith watching over her shoulder to see who it was.

Meredith heard Tara's agitated voice from the doorway. The voice on the other side of the door was male, and not a voice Meredith recognized. She rose quickly and peered over Tara's shoulder. The face she saw was the last face she expected to see at her door.

It was Peter. He looked angry and irritated, and he was trying to enter the room. Tara turned to Meredith, her eyes wide, wondering what to do.

"It's okay, Tara," Meredith told her. "Peter, come in. What's going on?"

Peter stalked in, and Tara closed the door behind him. Peter walked briskly until he was facing Meredith, standing mere inches from her. He looked down at her, unfazed by the fact that he had interrupted her on her wedding day, that she was standing before him in her white gown, ready to marry his brother-in-law.

He said, "What the hell are you doing?"

Meredith's jaw dropped. She realized that she had never heard Peter speak before; that was why she had not recognized the voice on the other side of the door. She hesitated before responding, unable to believe she had heard him correctly.

"Excuse me?"

"Meredith," he said. "I like to think I'm a good judge of character. I watch people carefully. I can have people pegged pretty quickly. But you I just don't understand."

Meredith was speechless. Her gaze shifted to Tara. Tara was staring at Peter, as shocked as she herself was.

"I'm not sure I know what you mean."

Peter sighed, impatient. "You always struck me as smart. You certainly seemed smarter than any of Shane's other girlfriends. That's what makes this so incredible to me."

Meredith's heart was pounding. She was so confused she couldn't even be insulted. Out of the corner of her eye she saw Tara approach her until she was standing by her side.

"Peter," Meredith said, trying to remain calm, "you're going to need to tell me what you're talking about."

Peter shook his head, his expression growing more annoyed by the moment. "I'm talking about you and Shane. I'm talking about you marrying into this godforsaken family. Meredith, I realize this is hard for you to hear, but I'm here to tell you that if you know what's good for you, you'll take off that dress, call off this wedding, and run, as fast as you can, away from Shane and all of the Thayers."

Meredith exhaled sharply, not believing what she was hearing. Tara placed her hand on the back of her shoulder.

"Why would you say such a thing?" Meredith exclaimed, beginning to panic. "I'm getting married in less than one hour!

Even if you have a reason to be telling me this, why would you wait until now to do it?"

"I would have told you sooner, but I was curious to see how long it would be before you figured it out. I never imagined that you were so foolish as to take it this far."

Meredith and Tara looked at each other, stumped. Meredith was at a loss for words. Tara spoke on her behalf.

"Could you be a little more specific? You can't just walk in here and say this without giving an actual reason."

"Meredith," Peter said, closing his eyes momentarily, then opening them and looking at her. His expression had softened. "Shane doesn't care about you. He's only marrying you to annoy his parents. He's been pushed around by them for years. This is his way of getting back at them, by showing them he won't be bossed around."

"What are you talking about?" Meredith cried. "Shane defended me when the senator brought up my father's editorial. He's marrying me in spite of the fact that his parents don't like my father."

"Don't you see? He's marrying you *because* they don't like your father—not in spite of it. Why do you think he was so impatient to marry you? Why do you think he proposed after only two months?"

Meredith's heart dropped. She was beginning to feel numb. She shook her head, as if denying it could make it not true.

"And speaking of patience," Peter went on, "I hear you've been grateful to him for not pressuring you to sleep with him. Oh yes, I know all about that too," he said curtly in response to Meredith's widening eyes. "Don't think for a minute Shane would be patient enough for your righteousness. What a joke. Are you really that naive?"

Meredith stared at him, speechless.

"What does he care if you won't sleep with him, Meredith?

He's been sleeping with Caroline this entire time. He was with her last night."

"What?" Tara exclaimed. "That's impossible!"

"It's true," said Peter. "I know it for a fact. He's been sneaking around with her for years. The only reason he doesn't bring it out into the open is that her father would cut off her money train. Also he likes the idea of holding his mother hostage," he added with a smirk. "Tess has been trying to get them together for years. Shane won't openly do anything his mother wants him to do."

Meredith was breathing heavily and thought she might faint. She closed her mouth and attempted to control herself. She fortified her face and looked at Peter carefully. "I need to talk to Maribel," she said. "There's no way what you're saying is possible. Maribel will straighten it out."

Peter laughed. "You really are clueless. Maribel knows all about it, Meredith. She talks around me as if I'm not even there. How do you think I know all this?"

Meredith was staring at the floor. She was trying to convince herself that Peter was wrong, but she knew he was telling the truth.

Finally she looked up at him. "Why are you here?" she asked. "What is the point in telling me this at all? Why do you care whether I marry Shane or not?"

"It's possible part of me feels sorry for you. But mostly I'm doing this because I detest the Thayers."

Tara had been rubbing Meredith's back, but her motion stopped at these words. Meredith turned to her, and Tara held her closer.

"Listen," Peter said. "I made the mistake of marrying into this family. They've made my life miserable. But you still have time to get out. Please do it. For your own sake." He studied her. "It's not worth it. Nothing is worth it."

The door swung open, and Maribel walked in. When she saw Peter standing there, her mouth opened with shock. Peter turned to look at her. His face expressionless, he walked by her and out the door, without casting Meredith another glance. Maribel watched him leave, then faced Meredith, not knowing whether to follow her husband or ask Meredith what was going on.

She decided to question Meredith. "What was that all about?" she asked, closing the door.

Meredith's eyes misted over with tears. "How could you do this? How could you let me marry Shane, knowing he's been seeing Caroline?"

Maribel's face turned white, and she folded her hands in front of her waist. "What?"

"Don't try to deny it," Tara told her. "Just tell her the truth."

Maribel lifted her chin in a gesture reminiscent of her mother. "He's my brother. I was just trying to help him."

"By lying to me?"

"Shane wants to marry you, Meredith. I wasn't going to do anything to prevent that from happening."

"I can't believe it," Meredith said softly, shaking her head. "You're just like them."

Maribel stood still, her chin lifted, her eyes on the floor. "I'm sorry," she said, though there was no sympathy in her voice. "I didn't want to hurt you. But as I said, he's my brother. I did what I had to do."

"Please leave," Tara told her. "Leave us alone."

Maribel was motionless for a moment, then turned and left.

Tara faced Meredith and sat her down on a chair. She knelt beside her and held her hand.

"Honey, I don't know what to say," she whispered. "What can I do for you?"

Meredith turned to Tara.

"Go get Shane."

～

MEREDITH STOOD by the window gazing onto the beautiful open field before her. She was motionless except for the rubbing of her hands, a mindless, repetitive gesture that gave away her anxiety.

There was a knock at the door.

"Come in," she called, forcing her voice to carry across the room.

The door opened, and Shane stepped in, wearing his tuxedo, ready to get married. He closed the door, then spotted Meredith at the window. Instantly his eyes grew wide, and his mouth dropped open. His face was overcome with an expression of wonder. His eyes roamed admiringly over her as he studied every detail of her in her dress, her face soft with emotion and her hair a delicate bundle on top of her head, her veil cascading down her back. He lost his breath, and his entire body tensed.

"Christ," he whispered.

Meredith felt tears rise but held them back, tightening her jaw in an effort to remain strong. She turned away from him.

"You look amazing," he said breathlessly from behind her.

She looked at him once more, a dark frown on her face. He sensed her agitation and stepped toward her.

"What's the matter?" he asked. "Tara said you wanted to see me." A mild smile crossed his face. "You know it's bad luck to see each other before the wedding."

"It's too late for that, Shane."

Abruptly his smile disappeared, and Meredith knew that he knew. "What do you mean?" he asked, but his attempt to appear ignorant was unconvincing.

"I know you've been sleeping with Caroline. And I know you're only marrying me to upset your parents."

When she mentioned Caroline, his expression remained unchanged; clearly he had been prepared for her to say that. But at her second statement, his eyebrows rose, and his face took on a defiant look.

"No, that's not true," he insisted. "Who told you that?"

"It doesn't matter," she replied, holding back her emotion with effort. "Shane," she said, her voice shaking as the tears threatened to break through. "How could you do this?"

"Meredith, please," he said, and held out his hands. "Look, I'll admit it, okay? At first I liked the idea of pissing off my parents. When I found out who your father is, it seemed perfect. But once I got to know you, all that changed. I meant everything I said about wanting to try. Come on, you have to believe me. I swear I'm telling the truth."

Meredith watched him and hated herself for believing him. She remembered all the times he had told her what a nice person she was, that he wanted to try to make her happy but wasn't sure he'd be able to.

"What about Caroline?" she asked.

His expression changed, and he became defensive. "Well, what did you expect, after all that time? Can you blame me?"

Meredith was disgusted. "Oh, Shane. You can't be serious."

"And anyway, what does it matter? We weren't married yet. I would have stopped seeing her after the wedding."

"Don't add insult to injury."

Shane's face softened, and he sat on the nearest chair, his elbows resting on his knees and his face blank as he stared into space. Meredith was reminded of Jason Richter, who had denied his wrongdoing and defended his behavior every step of the way. She pitied Shane as she looked at him in this light, as if he were a frightened child who had been caught with his hand in the cookie jar.

"I fucked up," he said, lifting his face, his eyes meeting hers. "I was weak. I'm sorry." He frowned, holding back his own emotion. "I didn't mean to hurt you."

Meredith wiped a tear from her eye and turned away from him. "I know you didn't."

From behind she heard his voice: "Are we still getting married?"

She turned back to face him. For the first time, she noticed how handsome he looked in his tuxedo and remembered how she had looked forward to the night they were supposed to have together.

She said nothing, but her face gave away her answer.

He looked down.

Meredith was staring at him. She knew that he was thinking that he had failed again, that he was wondering why happiness always seemed to elude him. Strangely, they had a lot in common, and she felt sorry for him in spite of her anger.

But she had had enough. "I think you'd better go," she said. "I'm now left with the task of letting everyone know there's not going to be a wedding."

He nodded, stood, and began to step toward the door. Abruptly he turned back to face her.

"Congratulate your golden boy for me."

Meredith was surprised. "What do you mean?"

"Wes was pretty sure it wouldn't last. He seemed to think he'd just wait it out and then sweep you back up. It looks like he won."

Meredith once again found herself speechless, and she watched as Shane walked to the door. When she realized he was going to leave without another word, that he was about to dismiss their entire relationship and the life they were supposed to have together, she was infuriated.

"Don't you have anything else you want to say to me?" she called to him.

He turned toward her and paused to consider.

"Yes," he said. "I'm sorry I'm such a screw-up."

He walked out of the room, leaving Meredith alone.

MEREDITH STARED out the passenger's side window of her car.

She was on her way back to Lovelace. She would be spending another night there after all.

Tara was driving. After the wedding had been called off and the families dealt with, Tara had insisted that she accompany Meredith home so they could think in peace. Vince had wanted to join them. Meredith had thanked him but told him to stay with her parents, that they needed his comfort and reason, as did she: she needed him to calm them down and try to mollify them. They had warned her about Shane, had begged her not to marry him; she had insisted that she knew best, and she had hurt herself and them in the process. She knew she had disappointed them once again.

Meredith allowed herself to recall the events of the day. She closed her eyes. She was ashamed of herself for letting her pain misguide her, for in the process she had lost her integrity, deliberately choosing not to see the facts that were right in front of her. She knew that Peter had been right, that Shane had not loved her. What Shane had loved was the fact that she was there, that she was trusting enough to give him a chance. She had stuck by him when no one else had. She had been nothing more than an opportunity to prove himself. He had been drawn to her sincerity, but anyone could have filled her role. Anyone could have been his wife.

Once again she had failed. Once again she had misjudged people. Once again she was starting fresh, only this time she had no job, no home, and parents who were beyond angry with her. She felt she had burned all her bridges. She didn't know what to do next. All this time she had thought her experiences had made her stronger and wiser; as it turned out, she was just as lost as ever and had nothing to show for any of it. But one thing she did know was that from now on she would be her own savior. Tara had been right. It was better to be alone than to be with a man she did not love. Even if it meant being alone for the rest of her life, she would never settle again. The alternative was the loss of her integrity. Anything was preferable to that.

It did not seem to matter what her strategy was, whether she stayed on the path before her or strayed from it; she was hurt every time. For the first time in her life, she considered that she might never find what she was looking for. She had come so close. She had been standing in her wedding dress, had finally felt safe. And yet the universe had found a way to disappoint her still. With horror she realized that the universe had nothing to do with it. Meredith had willfully deceived herself this time. It was her own fault.

She once again wondered where the tears were. She was worried about herself. The only thing scarier than being hurt was being hurt but not feeling the pain.

TARA TREATED Meredith as if Meredith were an ill patient, bringing her food and tea and tucking her into blankets. She sat with her, talking when Meredith wanted to talk and remaining silent when Meredith wanted to sit in silence. Meredith knew one day she would be able to thank Tara. For now she once again let her friend do her job, vowing to one day pay her back for saving her so many times.

The two friends discussed Meredith's options. Meredith saw only one thing to do. She had to return to her parents' house in Pennsylvania. There was no other way. Tara tried to insist that Meredith stay with her, but Meredith wouldn't hear of it. She would be enough of an imposition on her parents; she certainly did not want to impose on Tara and her family. She already felt herself to be enough of a burden. She didn't want to make it worse than it already was.

She dreaded going back to her parent's house; she felt almost sick when she thought of it. But she had mere weeks until she would be forced to move from this quiet house outside Washington, and she had no job. She had the little she had saved, but it was nothing that could sustain her for any length of time. Shane had been her future. As long as she married him, she would have had time to figure out what she was going to do. Now that he was gone she had nothing, and no time.

Early Sunday morning, Meredith and Tara climbed into Meredith's car to begin the drive toward Philadelphia. Meredith left her books and other random belongings, bringing only a small bag of clothing; she intended to return after a couple of weeks of contemplation. She couldn't deal with it all right now. She needed to feel as if she at least had a place of respite other than her parents' cold home.

Before she left, though, Meredith had one more thing to do. That morning, while Wes was playing tennis, she walked across the street toward the house she had grown to know so well, in which she had felt so much love and comfort. She stuck a letter in his door for him to find when he returned home.

The letter read:

Dear Wes,

I didn't marry Shane. You were right; I didn't love him. Also, he didn't love me. He was using me as a weapon against his parents, and he was cheating on me. I'm going back home to stay with my parents until I can figure out what my next step should be.

I haven't tried to hide the fact that my feelings for you never went away. You and I have a bond that isn't found every day. If I told you I wanted to be with you, that the idea of marrying you and living forever with you was now more appealing than ever— what would you do? Would it be enough, or would our differences still come between us? I think you want to be with me too, and I think in theory you would do anything to make it happen. But in order for us to be together, I need you to understand why I left in the first place. I need you to let me have my say when it comes to making decisions that affect us both. I need you to accept that I can be my own person and love you at the same time. I need you to see that by attempting to control my every move, by trying to hold me so tightly, you will actually drive me away.

If you can do all this, if you think you truly understand what I have been trying to tell you and feel strong enough to act on it, come to Philadelphia and bring me back to you. I will go willingly and joyfully.

No matter what happens, though, please know that I will always love you for you. I will always love you as a friend.

Meredith

To be continued ...

MEREDITH WITH THE WAVES

After overcoming heartache and loss, Meredith finds herself reveling in a life she once only imagined. Nestled into a peaceful existence with the love of her life, she looks forward to a future full of meaning and purpose. Newfound happiness makes it easy to find the strength to meet fresh challenges—building a new career, caring for her ailing father-in-law, and longing for her husband, whose work takes him far from home. It's clear to her that true growth lies not in the absence of adversity but in how she faces it.

But life has a way of testing even the strongest resolve. Increasing tension with her demanding parents, the emotional toll of a high-risk pregnancy, and the challenges of new motherhood all bring her face to face with the full weight of her past insecurities. And sudden upheaval in her husband's job makes true partnership and understanding that much more urgent.

Each hurdle forces her to confront her deepest fears and to finally grapple with the lessons life's been trying to teach her, pushing her to embrace the imperfections in her family, her life, and herself.

The final installment of the *Meredith* series, *Meredith With the Waves* is a poignant exploration of resilience, acceptance, and the complexities of human relationships. It's about the power of facing obstacles with courage and grace—and about how life's uncertainties hold the key to unlocking our inner strength and to understanding the true essence of happiness.

ALSO BY AMANDA GALE

Meredith Out of the Darkness

Meredith Against the Wind

Meredith With the Waves

Love in the Lavender

Strawberry and Sage

Sweet Lavvy

Catherine and the Wind

Gwyneth in the Garden

Maeve in the Morning

The Magic You Bring

Dahlia Almost Drowning

ACKNOWLEDGMENTS

My heartfelt gratitude goes to readers Melissa, Laura, Anna, Dez, Melissa, Erica, Jessica, Cindy, Bridget, Jennifer, Lasa, and Teresa.